I0702159

THE LIFE ONLY EXIST ON THE EARTH *
and
GOD CREAT EVE FROM RIP ADAM * 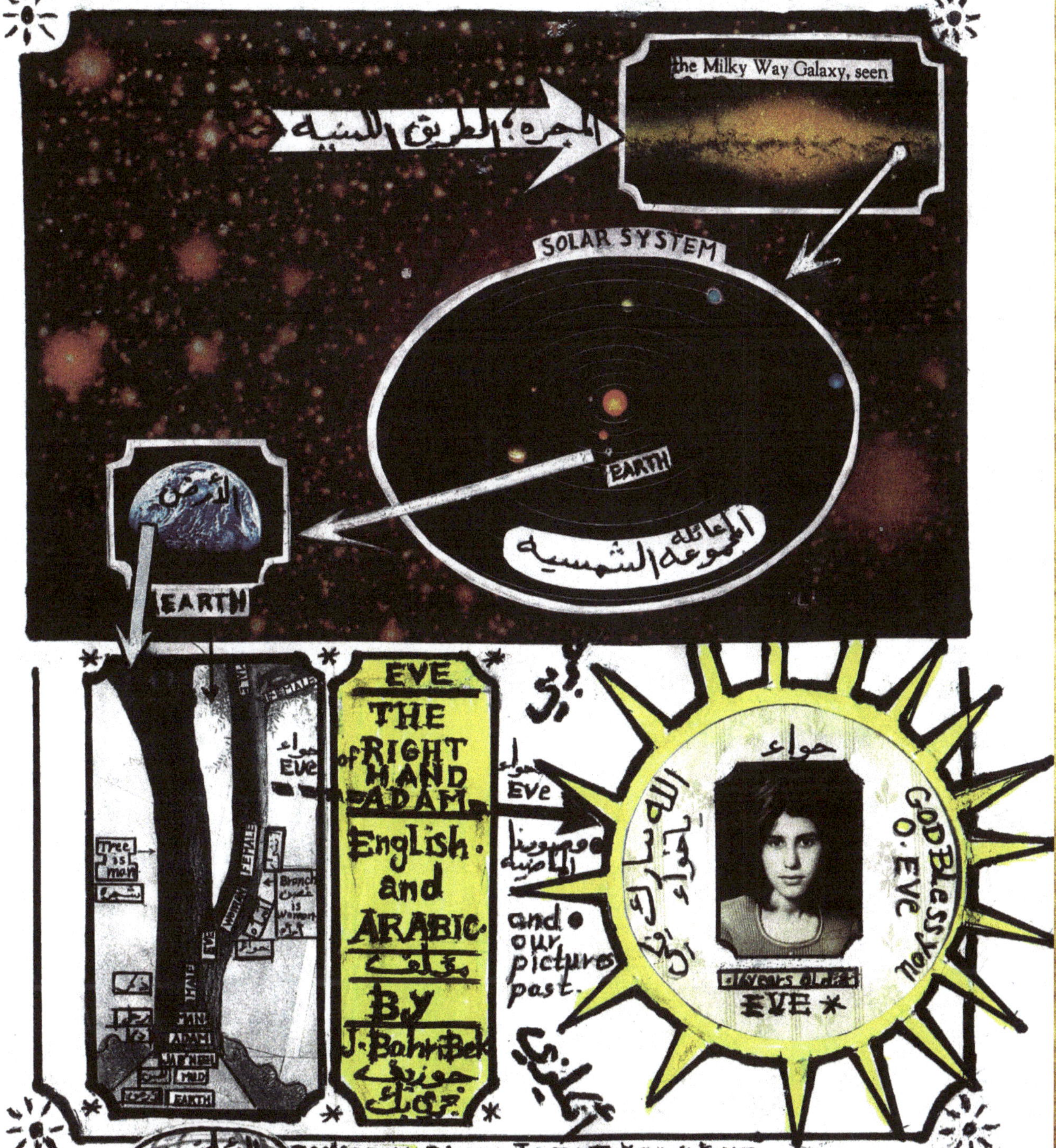
the Milky Way Galaxy, seen
SOLAR SYSTEM
EARTH
EARTH
EARTH
EVE
THE RIGHT HAND of ADAM
English and ARABIC
By J. Bahribek
Eve
and our pictures past.
GOD BLESS YOU
O. EVE
EVE
Books cover Disgn: J.E.B 2023

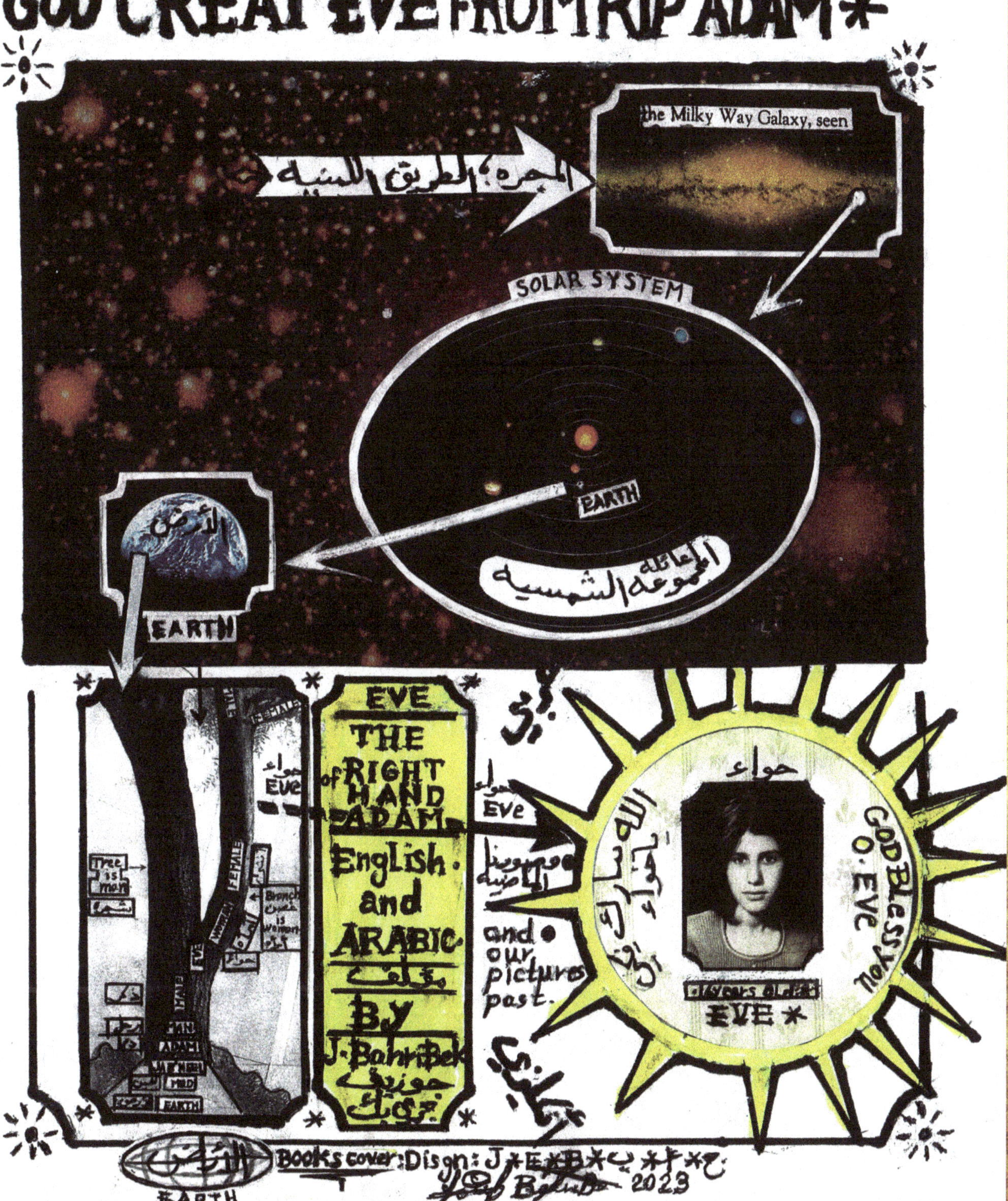
THE LIFe ONLY EXIST ON THE EARTH
and
GOD CREAT EVE FROM RIP ADAM *
I DO BELIVE GOD EXSIT
"Amen"
the Milky Way Galaxy, seen
SOLAR SYSTEM
EARTH
EARTH
EVE
THE RIGHT HAND of ADAM
English and ARABIC
By J. Bahri Bek
and our pictures past.
GOD BLESS YOU O. EVE
EVE
Eve
Tree is woman
Branch is Woman
ADAM
EARTH
Books cover Disgn: J.E.B 2023
EARTH

ARPress
45 Dan Road Suite 5
Canton MA 02021

Hotline: 1(888) 821-0229
Fax: 1(508) 545-7580

Ordering Information:

Quantity sales. Special discounts are available on quantity purchases by corporations, associations, and others. For details, contact the publisher at the address above.

Printed in the United States of America.

ISBN-13:   Paperback   979-8-89330-611-8

             eBook   979-8-89330-612-5

Library of Congress Control Number: 2024900548

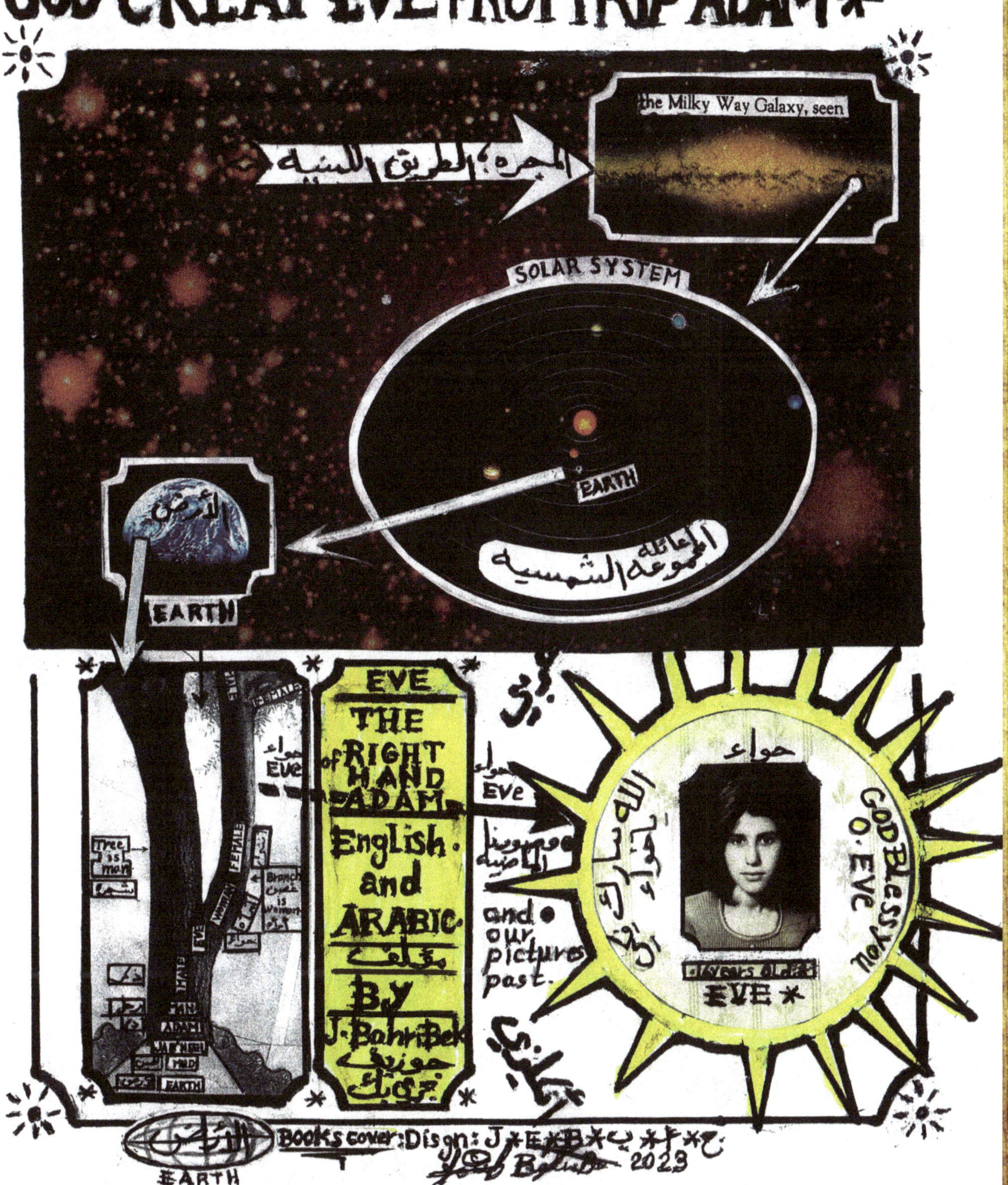

THE LIFe ONLY EXIST·ON THE EARTH*
and
GOD CREAT EVE FROM RIP ADAM *
I DO BELIVE GOD EXSiT ·Amen·
the Milky Way Galaxy, seen
SOLAR SYSTEM
EARTH
EARTH
EVE
THE RIGHT HAND of ADAM
English· and ARABIC
By J·BahriBek
EVE
GOD BLESS YOU
O. EVE
EARTH
BOOKS cover Disgn: J·E·B·
2023

1 ✓ INTRODUCTION

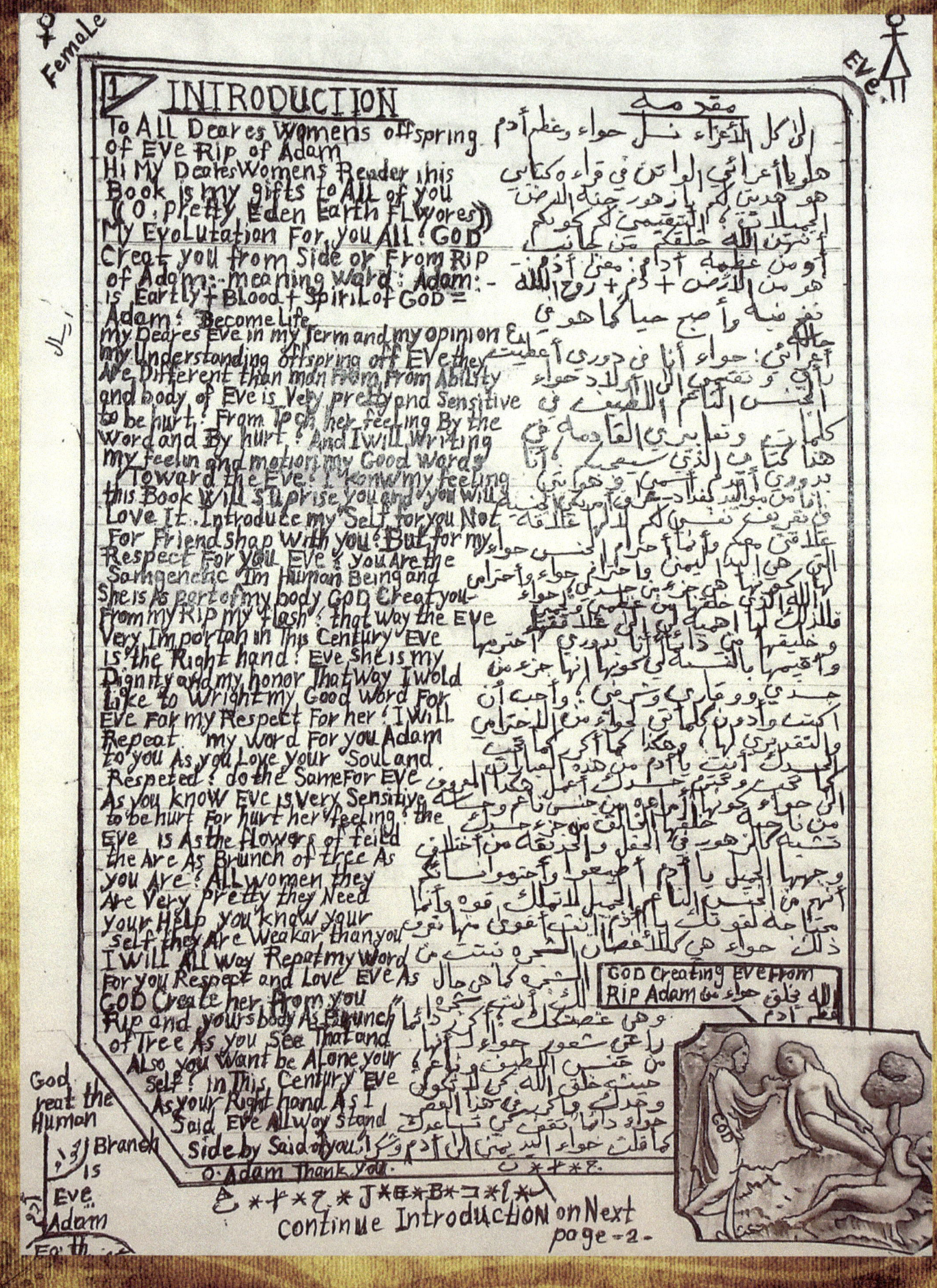

To All Deares Womens offspring
of Eve Rip of Adam
Hi My Deares Womens Reader this
Book is my gifts to All of you
((O, pretty Eden Earth FLwores))
My EvoLutation For you All? GOD
Creat you from Side or From Rip
of Adam:- meaning word: Adam:-
is Eartly + Blood + Spirit of GOD =
Adam? Become Life
my Deares Eve in my Term and my opinion
my Understanding offspring off Eve they
Are Different than man From From Ability
and body of Eve is Very pretty and Sensitive
to be hurt? From Ip oh her feeling By the
Word and By hurt? And I will Writing
my feelun and motion my Good word
    Toward the Eve? I konw my feeling
this Book Will suprise you and you will
Love It. Introduce my Self for you Not
For Friendshap With you? But for my
Respect For you Eve? you Are the
Samgenetic Im Human Being and
She is As part of my body GOD Creat you
From my Rip my flash? that way the Eve
Very Importan in This Century Eve
is the Right hand? Eve she is my
Dignity and my honor That way I wold
Like to Wright my Good word For
Eve For my Respect For her? I will
Repeat my word For you Adam
to you As you Love your Soul and
Respeted? do the SameFor EVE
As you know Eve is Very Sensitive
to be hurt For hurt her feeling? the
Eve is As the flowers of feild
the Are As Brunch of tree As
you Are? ALL women they
Are Very pretty they Need
your Help you know your
self they Are Weakar than you
I Will All way Repat my word
For you Respect and Love EVE As
GOD Create her from you
Rip and yours body As Brunch
of Tree As you See That and
Also you want be Alone your
self? in This Century Eve
As your Right hand As I
Said Eve All way stand
Side by Said of you
O. Adam Thank you.

Continue Introduction on Next page - 2 -

2

INTRODUCTION

From page -1-

My Deares Reader

This Book! All meaning my

Words Im Writing the Words

For you is From Holy Book

TORaH! old Testamet All

Sources is Right! been

Written in the BIBLE I call

Him Holy Notic Book

Which I mean All words of

Bible is Right and Holy words

in Bible in old Testament in.

Genesis. Genesise: 1:26-28 *

²⁶Then GOD Said, "Let Us

Make, man in Our Image, in our

Likenes, and Let the man RuLes

Ove the fish of Sea and the bird

of the Air, Over the live Stock,

Over all the Earth, and over

All Creatures: that move

aLong the grund ²⁷GOD

Created man in his own Image

in the Image of GOD he Created

him; maLe and femaLe Created them. ²⁸GOD

Blessed them and Said to them "Be fruitful &

Increase in number; fill the Earth and Subdue It.

J*⊞*�‿*‡*⩘*⊐*9
Tue * July * 25 * 2023
God Bless All
Woman
Amen

Female

Eve.

God Creat the Human

Branch is

EVE

Adam the Tree
Earth   ← the mo'her

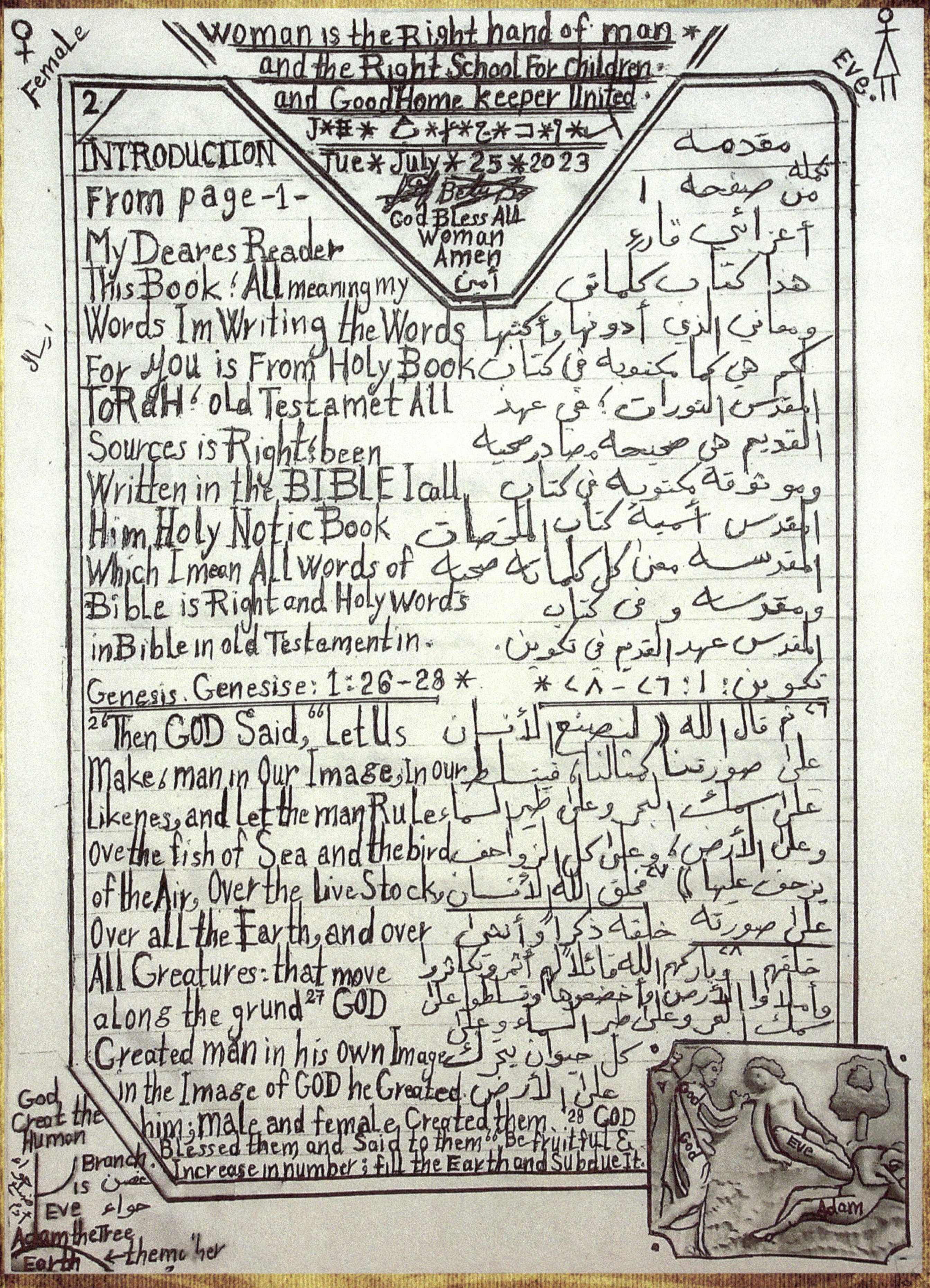

Female ♀

Eve ♀

J*E* △ *⨍*Չ*Ⴑ*⊐*٦

3

INTRODUCTION

continue From
Page-1 and 2

Genesis: 1: 28 - 29

Rule Over the fish of Sea
and Bird of the ☒ Air and Over Every Living
Creatur that moves On the Ground.

Tue * July * 25 * 2023

God Bless All
Woman
Amen
آمين

مقدمه

تكمله من صحه 1 و. ٢
تكوين : ١ . ٢٨ . ٢٩
في الأنكلزي

Genesis: 2 : 21 - 23 .

تكوين : ٢ : ٢١ – ٢٣ .

[21] So the LORD
GOD Coused the man to fall in to
Sleep, and While Closed Up the
place With flesh [22] Than the LORD
GOD made a Woman from the Riphcc
taken out of the man, and he brouht her
to the man. The man Said "This is Now
Bone of my Bones and flash of my flesh (body)
She Shall be Called Woman, for She Was taken out of Man.
Amen! and truth. * J*Ⅲ*B* *⊐*٩*⅄* *ʒ*⨍*ع*

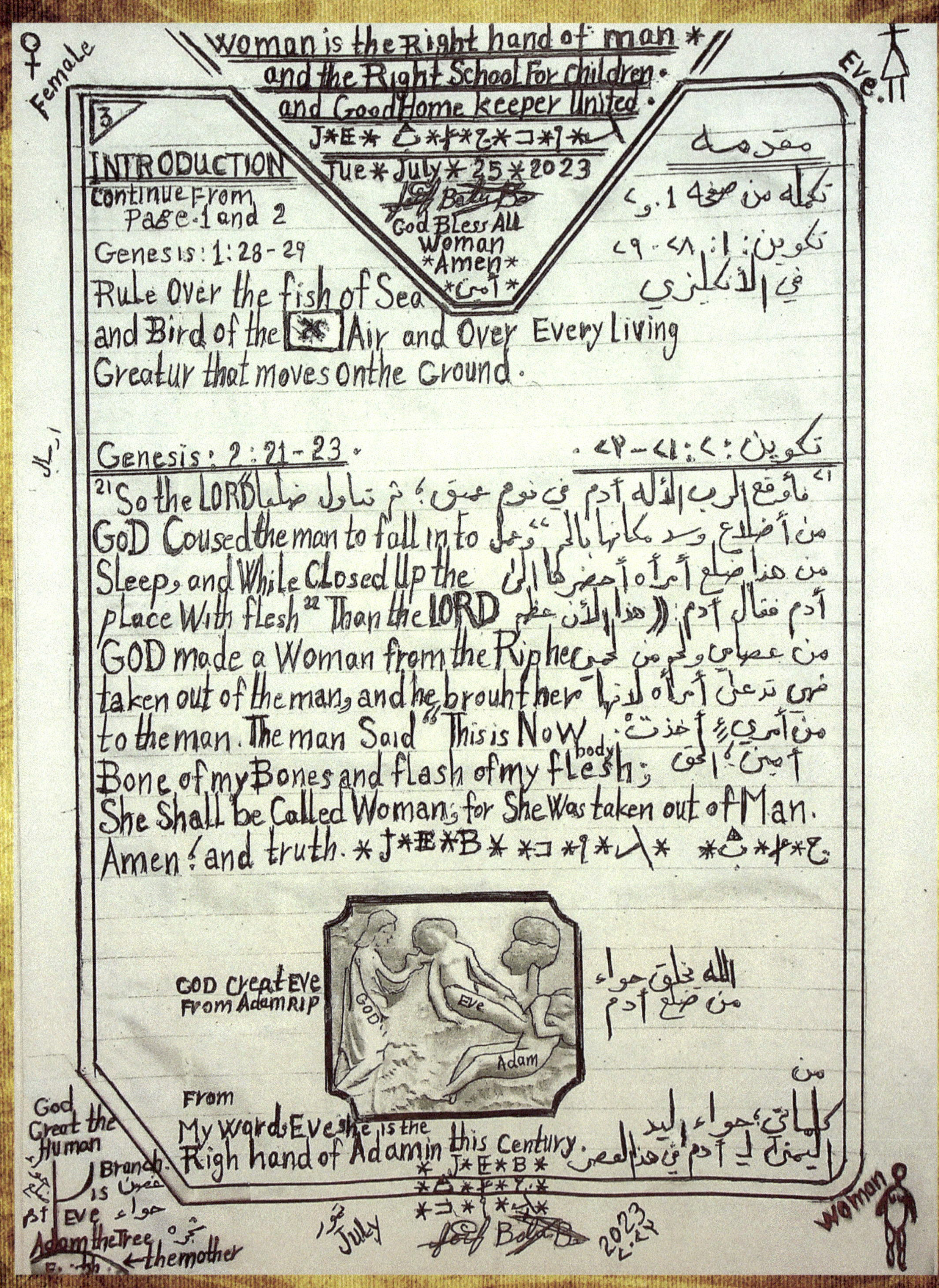

GOD creat EVE
From Adam R I P

الله يخلق حواء
من ضلع آدم

From
My word Eve she is the
Righ hand of Adam in this Century.
J * E * B
△⨍*Չ*

God
Great the
Human
Branch
is

Bt EVE حواء
Adam the Tree ←the mother

From
كل آتي، حواء، اليد
اليمنى لـ آدم في هذا العصر

July

2023

WOMAN ♀

④ INTRODUCION

مقدمه

Frome page 3

تكمله من صفحه ٣

It is Come from Shose that
dirt is pick the dirt and Enter It
in your Car. For Driving your
Car for Second Time, your
shose pick It (mass of Dirt)

That Way I WiLL Say For you
This probable "There" Nothing
By It Self Do that As it
is in that stats you pick It
Under your Shose to your
Car There is Nothing By It
Self Do That for it Self
If there is Second Thing
to Do With it As in Autom
Nuclis & Electron As in
the two hands It Want
Make Noise When your
hands claps. my Dear
I will Discontinue With my
Articles and my Words
For you my Notice: one Object
It CanNot meke Motion
or moving or phisics or
chemics If there is
is Not two Object As in
This ILLustrativ Drawing

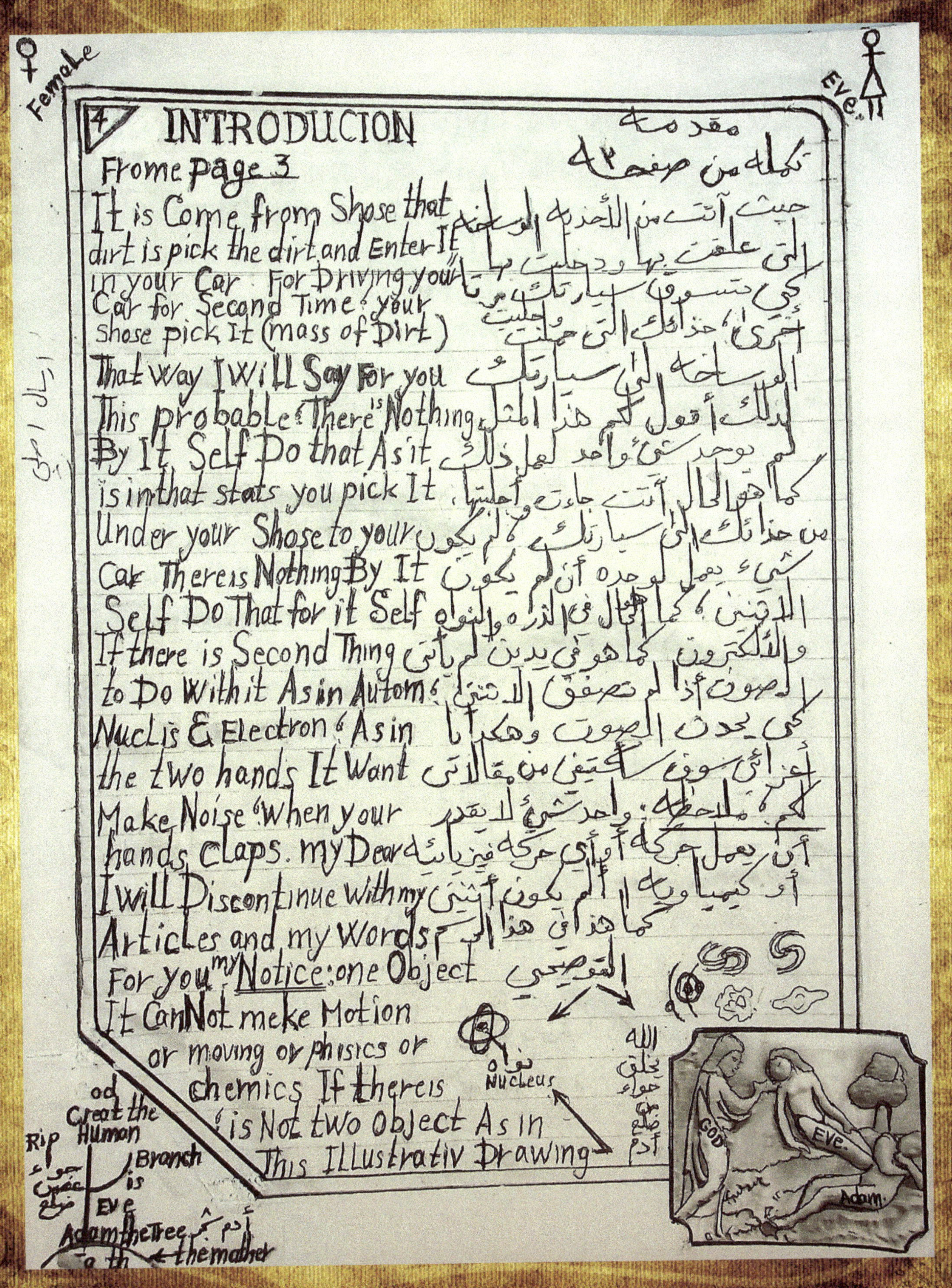

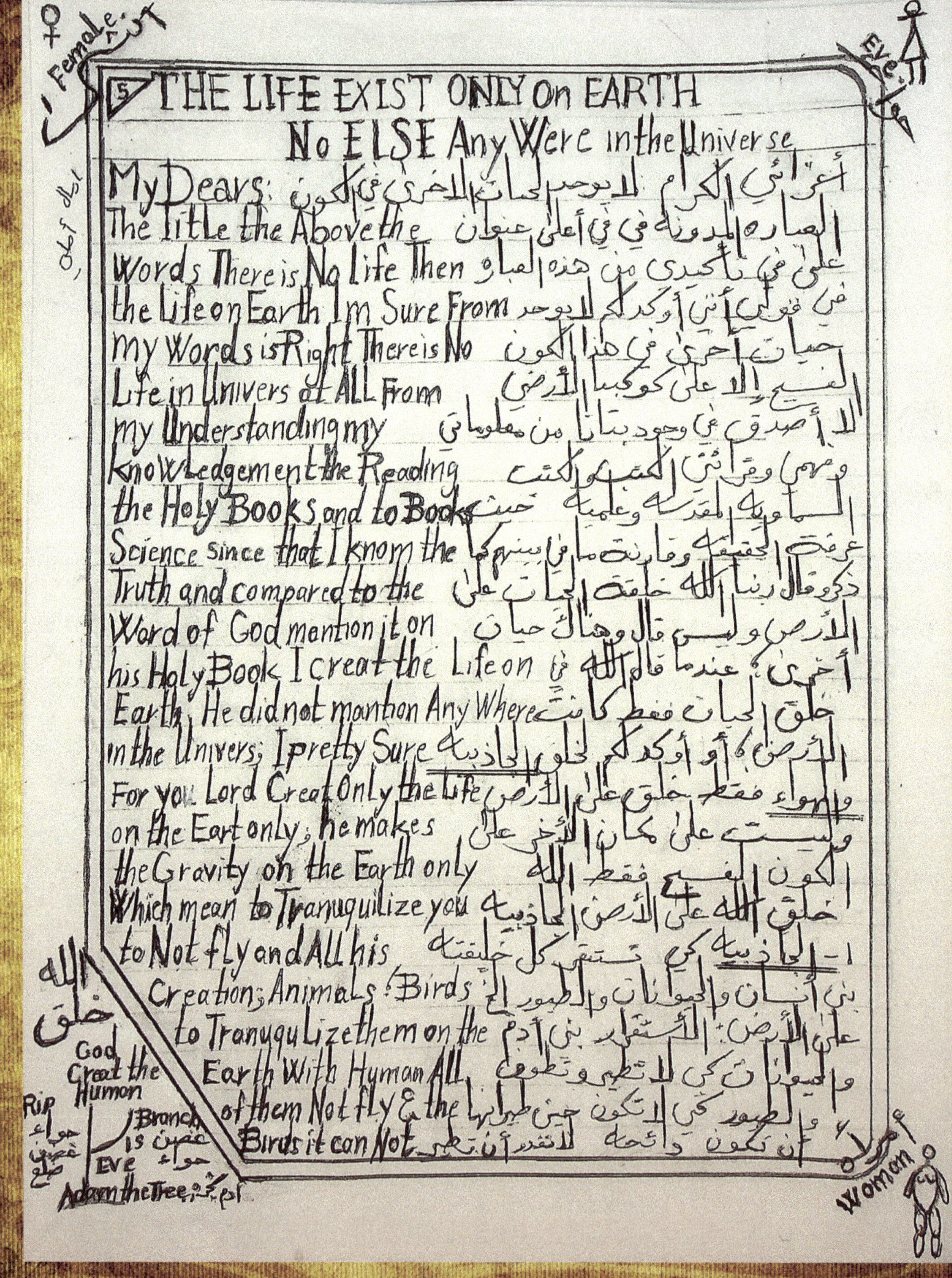
THE LIFE EXIST ONLY On EARTH
No ELSE Any Were in the Universe
My Dears:
The Title the Above the
Words There is No Life Then
the Life on Earth Im Sure From
my Words is Right There is No
Life in Univers at ALL From
my Understanding my
Knowledgement the Reading
the Holy Books and to Books
Science Since that I know the
Truth and compared to the
Word of God mention it on
his Holy Book I creat the Life on
Earth, He did not mantion Any Where
in the Univers; I pretty Sure
For you Lord Creat Only the life
on the Eart only; he makes
the Gravity on the Earth only
Which mean to Tranuquilize you
to Not fly and ALL his
Creation; Animals; Birds
to Tranuqulize them on the
Earth With Human ALL
of them Not fly & the
Birds it can Not
Female
Eve
God Creat the Humon
Rip
Branch is
Eve
Adam the Tree
Woman

THE LIFE EXIST ONLY On EARTH

continue From page 0

No ELSE Any Were in the Universe
to be Druggie When they flys and Hite
Each Other When they flys or
When you drink the Water they
Won't flays Like Bubble And
you cannot Drink It & put it in the
mouth it Begn to fly From your Mouth
Because No Cravity and you Cannot
Nursing the Animalis Becaus they
cannot be Tranuquilize they Will
flying From the Earth Because
there is No Cravity & Lord Creat the
Cravity on the Earth to Tranuquilize you & Belong to you on the
Earth that Way the Lord he
Creat Cravity & the Air is part the Life on
the Earth Not Else Where
in the Universe! & the Air
is maine Sources of the Life
For ALL Man kind & Animalis
my Dears When you
Read this Words is
Right Sources From
my Understanding & my
know Legement & my Reading
I Do Belleve 100% There is No
Life & Leave any Where ELse in Univers Just on Earth

THE LIFE EXIST ONLY On EARTH
No ELSE Any Were in the Universe

continue From page 6

Dear Value One

When you here From All Source
of the Life; or Any Creature of
of flying Saucer's As U.F.O.
Don't Believe It Just is Imgen-
tion or Superstition O Human-
bean As you Thinking a but It
Believe in My Words is Just is
is Spying Object Spying
Space Crfts; spying
on Each Other Or Just
As a Reflecting the Objct
or Telestars or Telecomunication (satelite, moons)
Moon is Reflection the (satelite, phenomena)
Light From them or Just
Words or Suprstions is No Sources
From been Exist This Object.
When Mighty Lord Said only
Great the Life on the Earth the
About the Oravity and the
Earth to tranuguil-
ze you on the Earth And
Else. & I will Say the Lord
have own, No measurement
or Scales. lord sone year
the Year is 1000
years Equal one
Days Earthly one the Earth is 24 hours

Female

EVE

God
Creat the
Human

RIP

EVE

Adam the Tree & rest

Branch
is

Woman

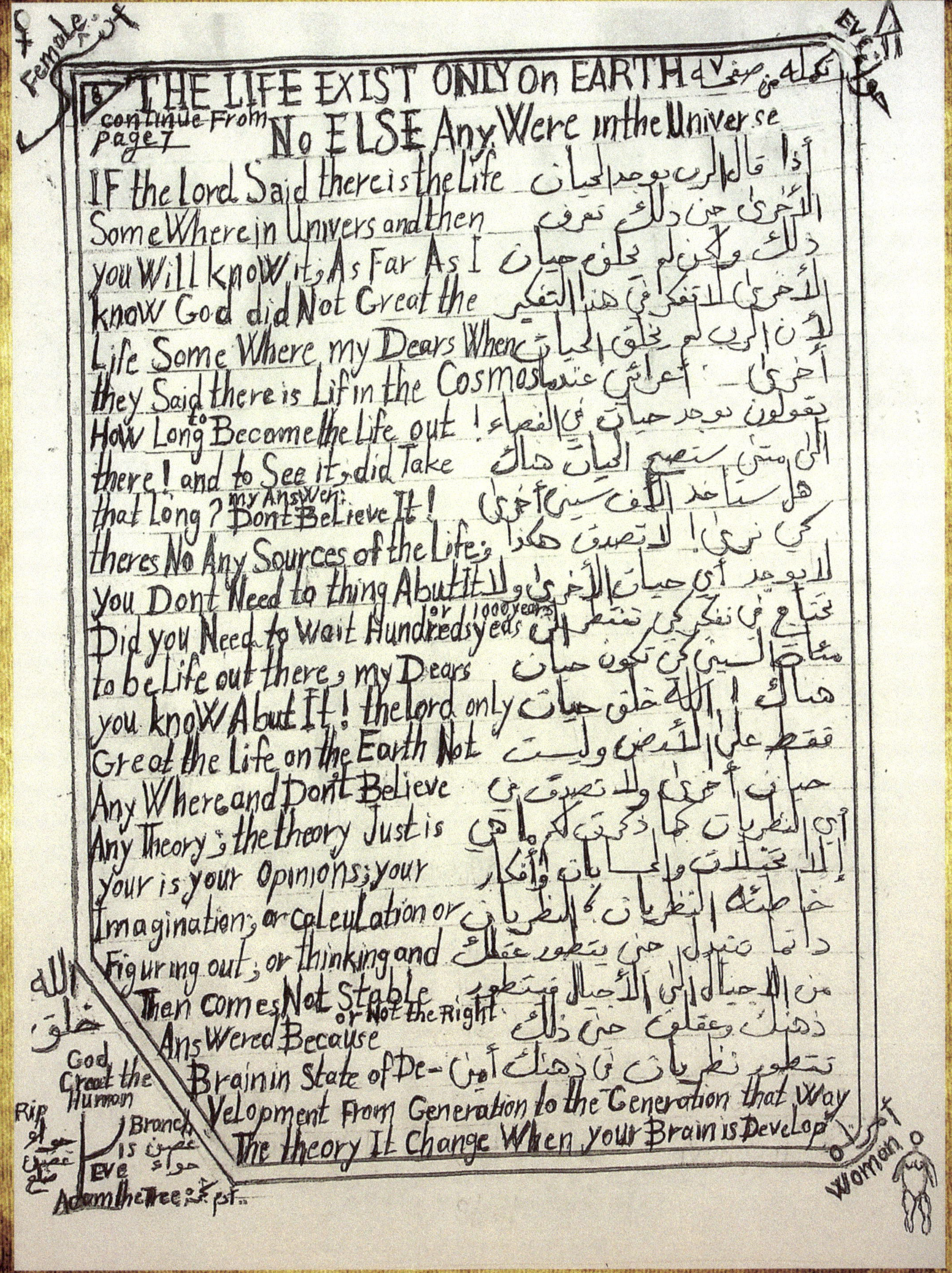

Female ♀
Eve
THE LIFE EXIST ONLY On EARTH NO ELSE Any Were in the Universe

continue From page 7

IF the Lord Said there is the Life
Some Where in Univers and then
you Will know it, As Far As I
know God did Not Great the
Life Some Where my Dears When
they Said there is Lif in the Cosmos
How Long to Became the life out
there! and to See it, did Take
that Long? my Answer: Dont Believe It!
theres No Any Sources of the Life;
you Dont Need to thing Abut It!
Did you Need to Wait Hundreds yeds or 1000 years
to be Life out there, my Dears
you know Abut It! the lord only
Great the Life on the Earth Not
Any Where and Dont Believe
Any Theory; the theory Just is
your is your Opinions; your
Imagination; or caleulation or
Figuring out; or thinking and
Then comes Not Stable or Not the Right
Answered Because
Brain in State of De-
velopment From Generation to the Generation that Way
The theory It Change When your Brain is Develop

God Great the Human
Rip
Branch is
Eve
Adam the Tree pst.
Woman ♀

9

* I DO BELIEVE GOD IS EXSITE
AND CREATED the UNIVERS EVERYTHING IN IT.

* أومن في وجود الله وخالق الكون الأشياء كل فيه

* BETWEEN ME AND HIM love IS NOT AS SEED OF MASTERD IS MORE Than That!
J*E*B*

بيني وبينه حب ليست حبة الخردل وأنا أكثر من ذلك
ع*ا*ب

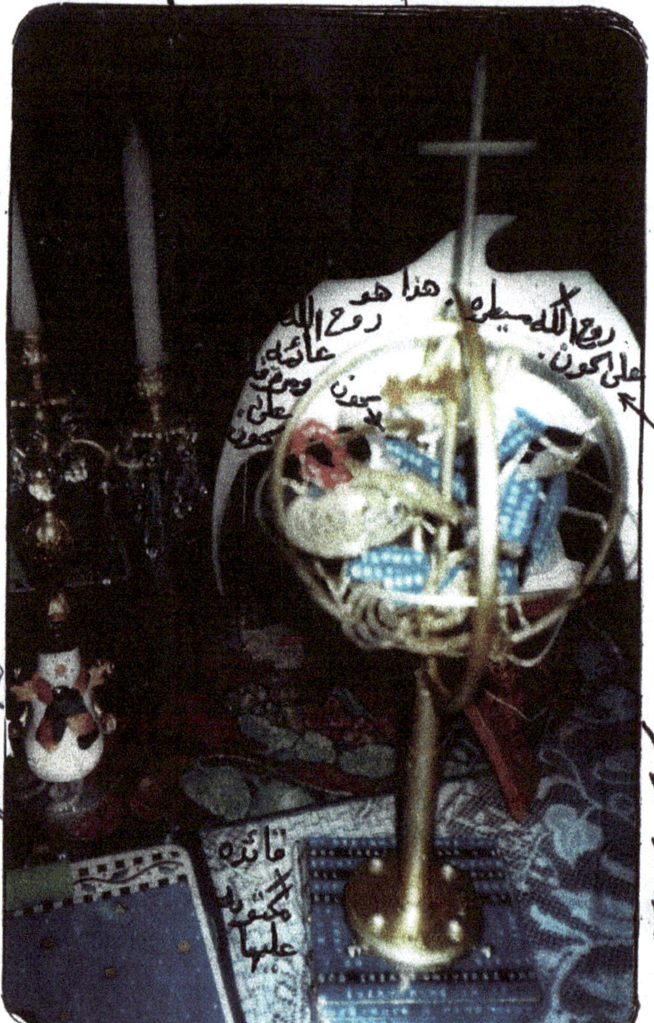

GOD SPIRIT HOVERING ON UNIVRES

بسم الله والابن والروح القدس الإله الواحد آمين
بسم الله الرحمن الرحيم آمين
أومن الحق
ع*ا*ب
J E B

In the Name the father and the Son and the Holy Spirit. Amen.
I Belive it. IS Truth.

MY HAND MADE UNEVRES
GOD Spirit HOVERING over
ALL UNIVERSE

نموذج الكون صنع من اليدي
روح الله ترفرف فوق
الكون

on year: Dec. 7 - 2007
في ٢٠٠٧ ٧/١٢/٢٠٠٧
J*E*B*ب*ا*ع

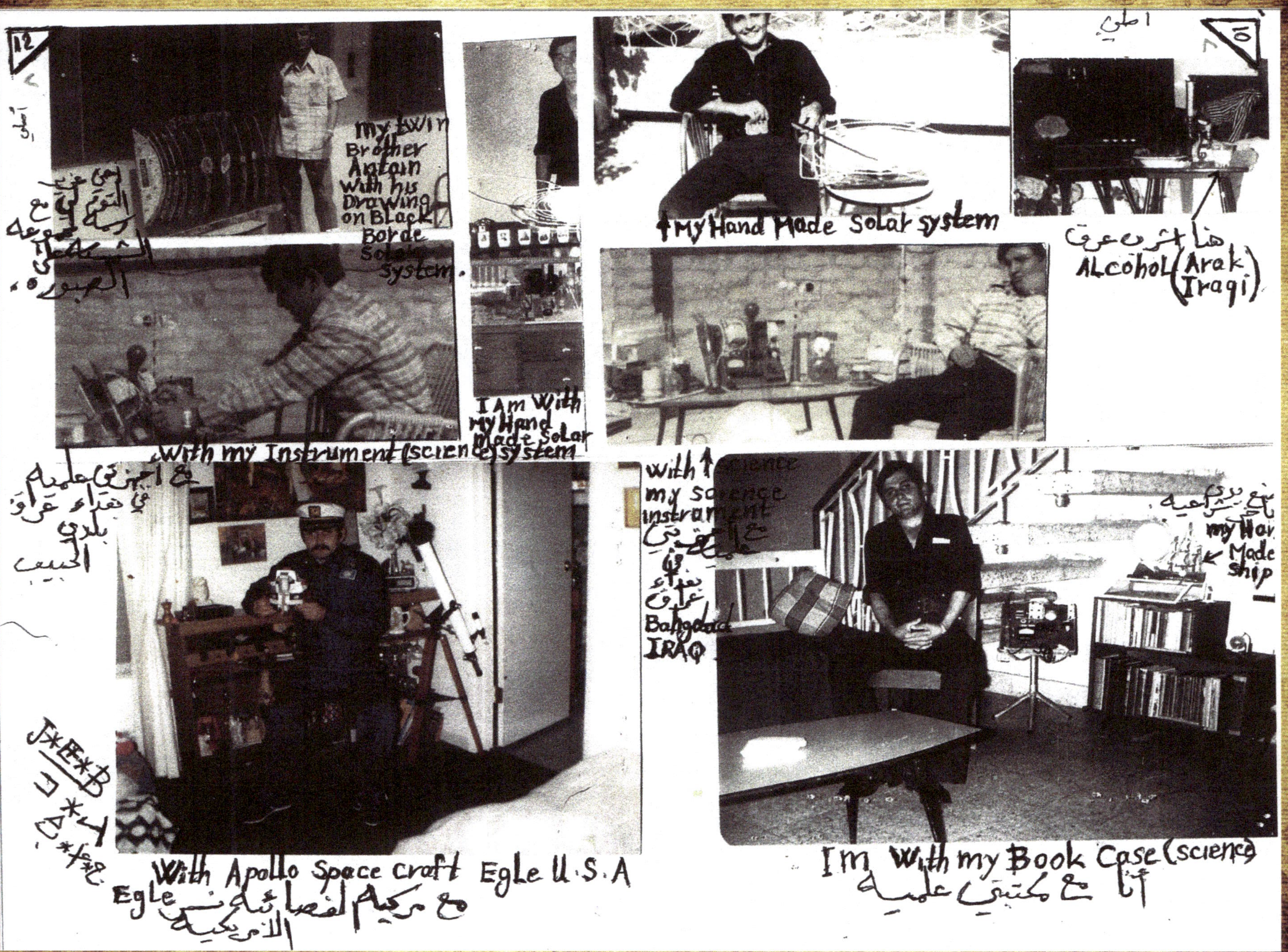

my twin Brother Antoin with his Drawing on BLack Bord Solar System.
↑ My Hand Made Solar system
هنا شرب عرق ALcohoL (Arak) (Iraqi)
I Am With my Hand Made Solar system
With my Instrument (science) system
with 1 science my science instrument
Baghdad IRAQ
↑ my Hand Made ship
With Apollo Space craft Egle U.S.A Egle
I'm With my Book Case (science)

أنا أمام تلسكوب الذي
صنعته في معرض معرض
الدولي الحائز على جائزة الدولة الأولى
في سنة ١٩٧١ - ١٩٧١
جوزيف إيشو جميل

بسم الله الرحمن الرحيم
الجمهورية العراقية

وزارة الشباب
مديرية الرعاية العلمية العامة
مديرية والجمعيات رائد الارصاد العلمية

العدد / ٧ / ٢٨٤
التاريخ / ٢٩ / ١٠ / ١٩٧١

الى / السيد لمجمع جمعة إميشتهر المحترم :-

يسرنا ابلاغكم بأن لجنة التحكيم قد وافقت على قبول مشاركتكم في المسابقة العلمية السابعة التي نظمتها مديريتنا وقد أحرز جهازكم المرتبة (أولى تلكسوب)
فيرجى مراجعة ديوان المديرية في شارع المغربي في بغداد يوم الجمعة الموافق ٢٩ / ١٠ / ١٩٧١ الساعة العاشرة صباحا لتسلم الجائزة · مع تقديرنا لجهودك وتمنياتنا لك بالموفقية ·

تلكوب غاليلو
يوسف ايشو بجري بك

كامل آدهم الدباغ
مدير الرعاية العلمية العام

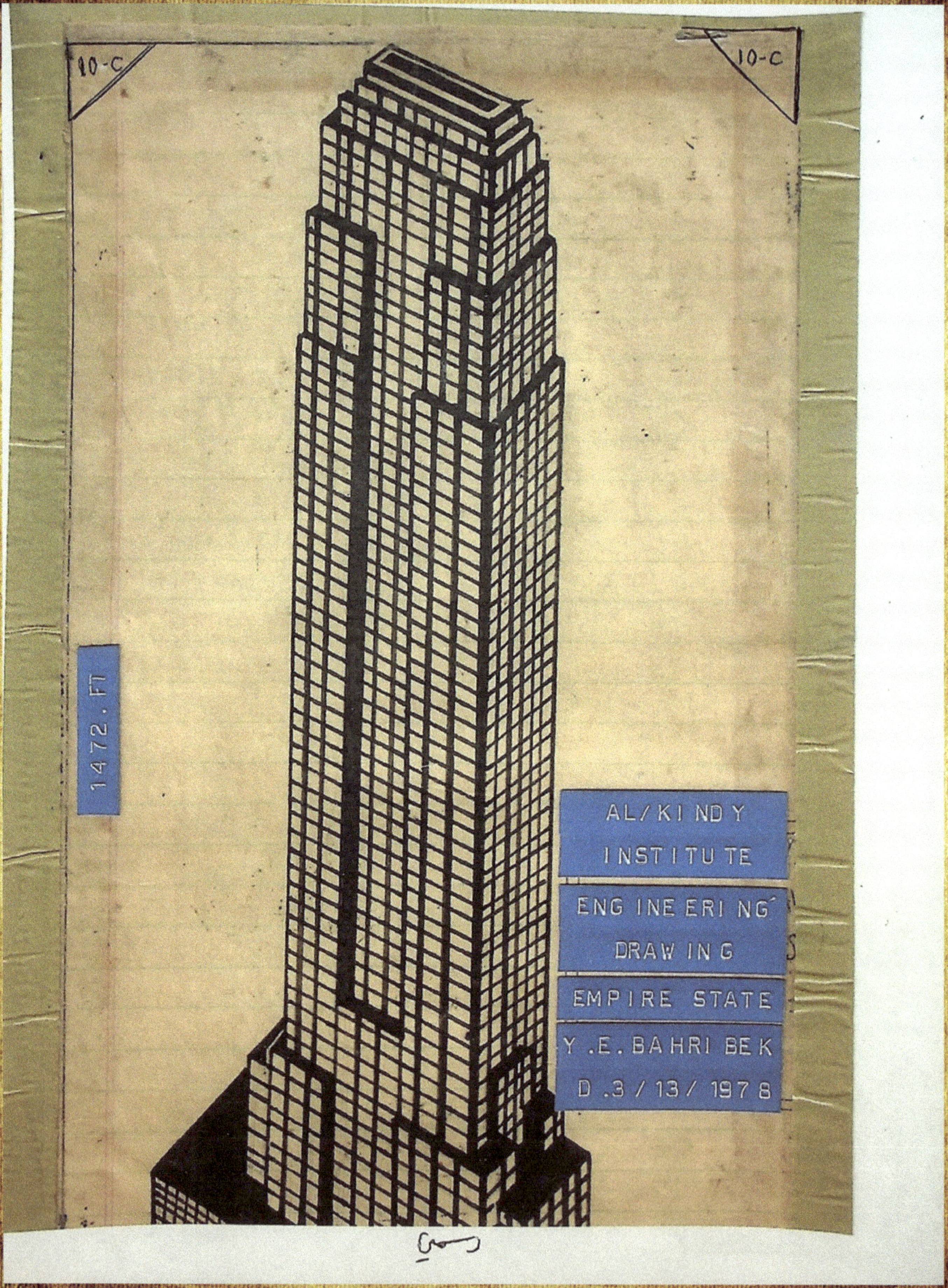

10-C
10-C
1472. FT
AL/KINDY
INSTITUTE
ENGINEERING
DRAWING
EMPIRE STATE
Y.E. BAHRI BEK
D .3 / 13 / 1978

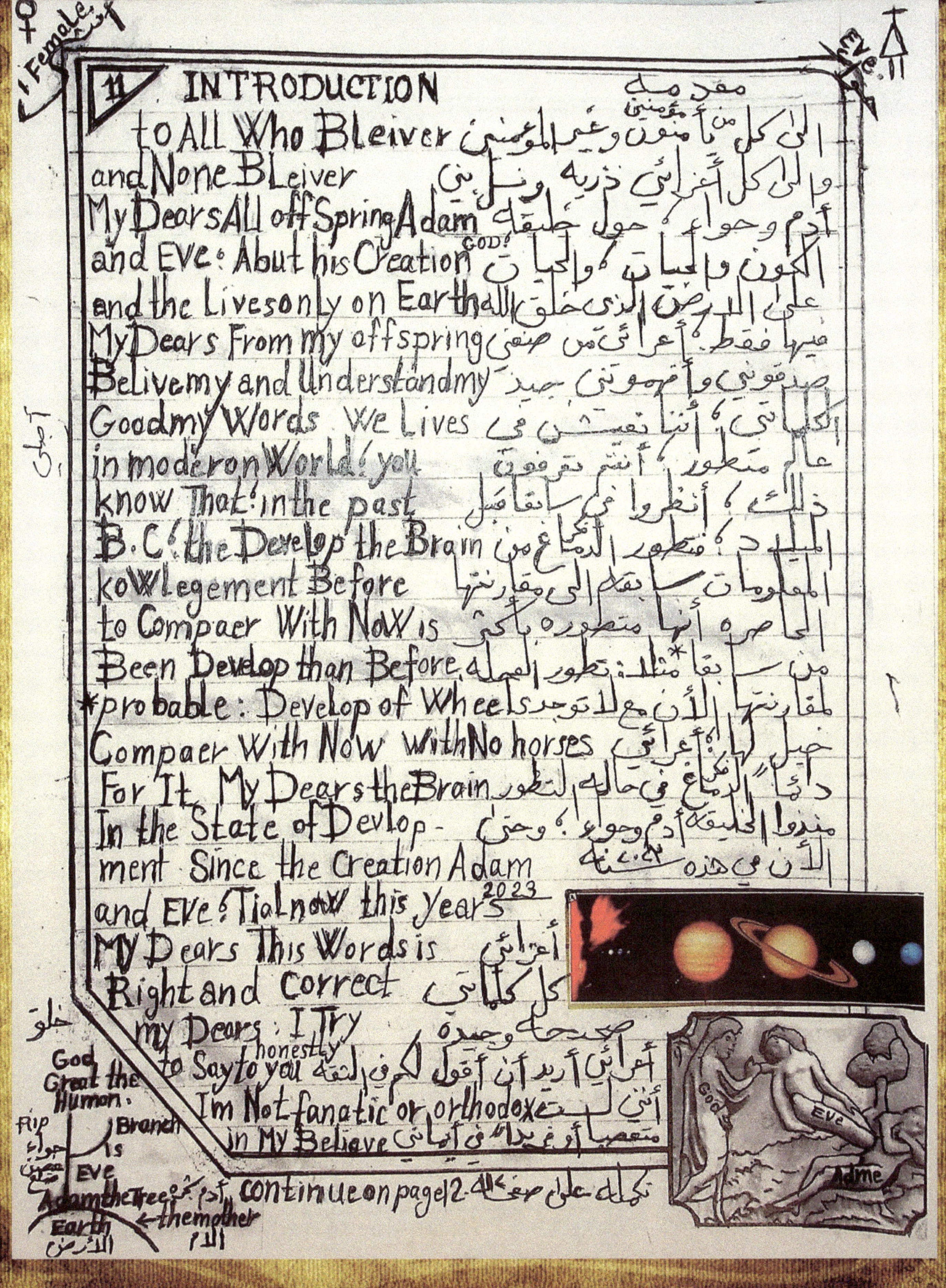

INTRODUCTION

مقدمة

to All Who Bleiver

and None BLeiver

My Dears ALL off Spring Adam

and EVE: Abut his Creation GOD!

and the Lives only on Earth all

My Dears From my offspring

Belive my and Understand my

Good my Words We Lives

in moderon World! you

know That! in the past

B.C! the Develop the Brain

koWlegement Before

to Compaer With Now is

Been Develop than Before.

*probable: Develop of Wheels

Compaer With Now with No horses

For It, My Dears the Brain

In the State of Devlop-

ment Since the Creation Adam

and EVE! Tial now this years 2023

My Dears This Words is

Right and Correct

my Dears: I Try

to Say to you honestly

I'm Not fanatic or orthodoxe

in My Believe

God Great the Humon.

FLIP

Branch is

EVE

Adam the Tree ← the mother

Earth الأرض

continue on page 2

INTRODUCITON

From page-1-

مقدمة
تكملة من صوحة 11-9

In My Beleive in GOD في أيماني أي بالله، هذه هي
This is my Realty and the Truth حقيقتي والحقيقة
my Dears All mankind I أعزائي بني البشر، أقول
I Will Say for you I Read a لقد قرأت كل الكتب العلمية
all Sciene Books and All و النظريات حول وحول
Theorys abut Evolution نشوع الكون والكيان على
The Univers and the Life on the Earth. الأرض
Believe in my Word the Theorys صدقوني في كل ما أن
you Read it, they Are is No النظريات كما قرأتوها
Right and No Currect ! إنها ليست صحيحة
As I mention It the كما ذكرتوا سابقا نظريات
Theorys All Ways can be دائما تتغير من التطور للفكر
Change the Develop the brain الدماغ قابل للتغير
* Do not Beleive in Theorys: لا تصدق في النظريات
Because Theory is Just لأنها ليست إلا ت أف ت وهي
is in your Thinking or Calculating wrong في تفكير أوحسابات
or figuring out or your Opinin أو تستنتج أو رأى أو تخيلت
or Imagenation All Words and كل هذه كلمات وأفكر ذكرية في
Lesson I mention It in كتابي لقاء
My Book Do you know W هل تعلم
posted at Amazon كما منشورة في

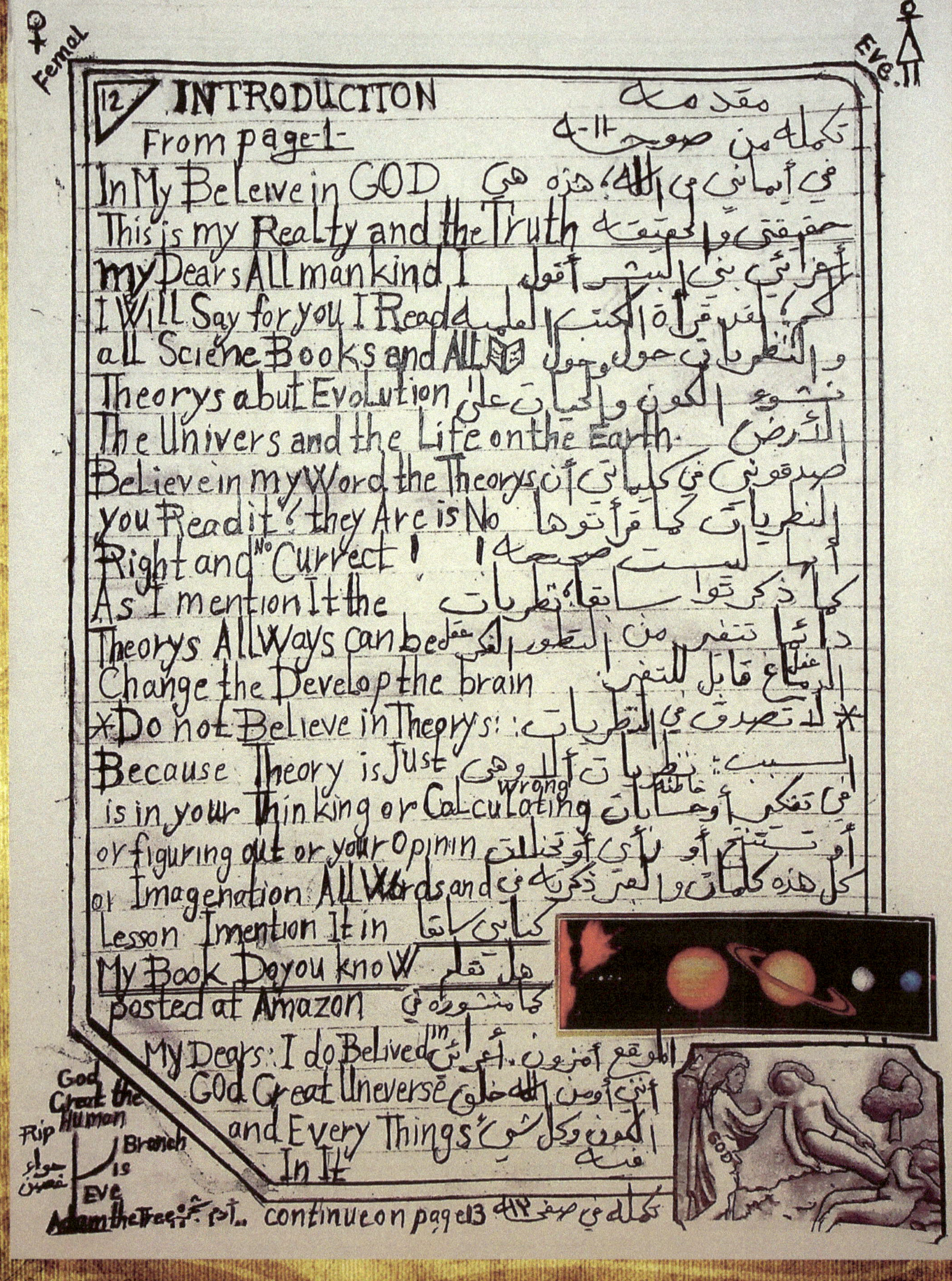

My Dears: I do Belived in الموقع أمزون، أعزائي
GOD Great Uneverse إني أومن بالله خلق
and Every Things الكون وكل شئ
In It فيه

Adam the Tree est. continue on page 13 تكملة في صفحة 13

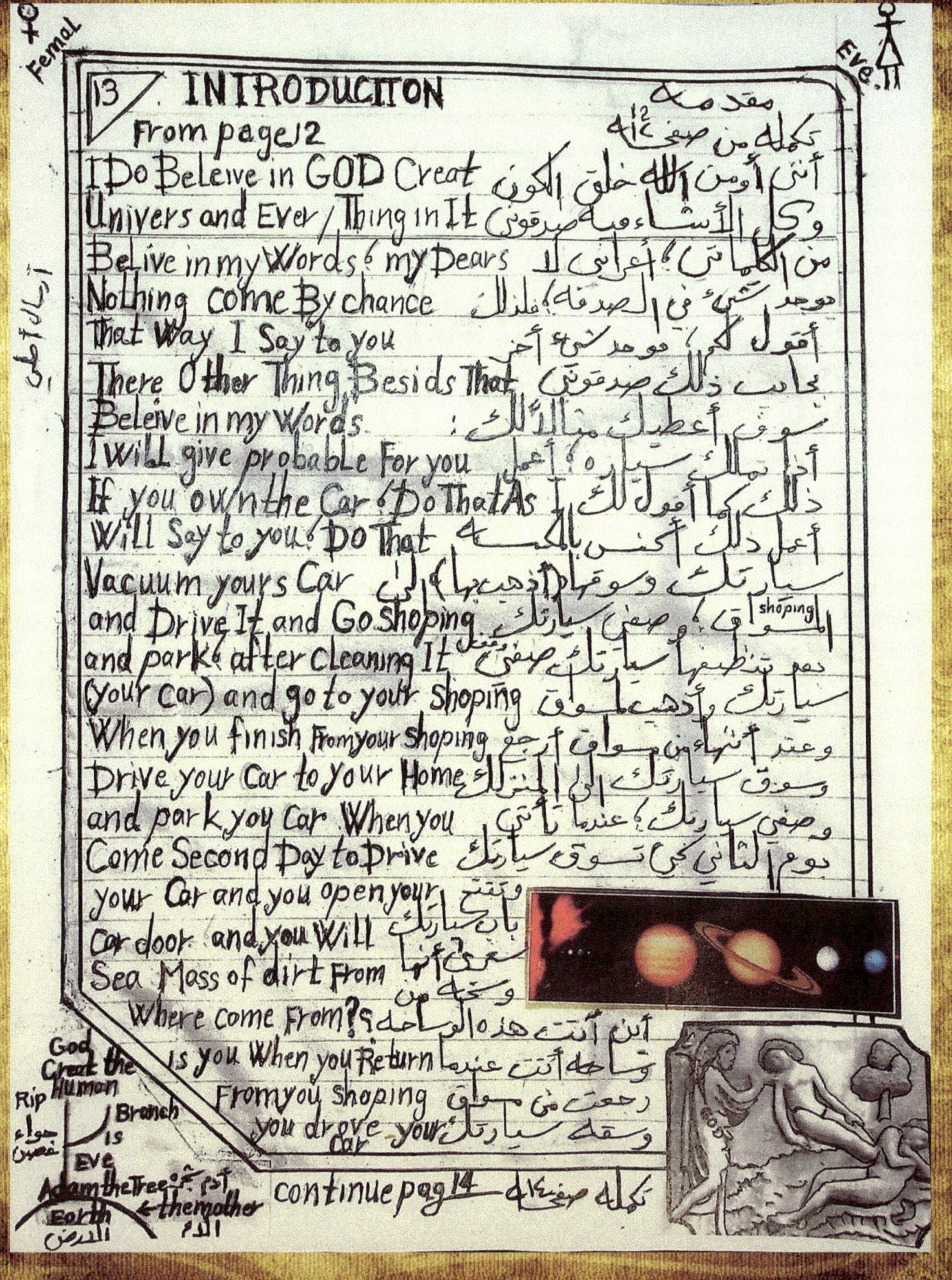

Femal
Eve.

13 / INTRODUCITON
مقدمه
تكمله من صفحه 12
From page 12
I Do Beleive in GOD Creat
انى اومن بالله خلق الكون
Univers and Ever / Thing in It
وكل الاشياء ميه صدقونى
Belive in my Words, my Dears
من الكلمات، اعزانى لا
Nothing come By chance
يوجد شى فى الصدفه، فلذلك
That Way I Say to you
اقول لكم، يوجد شى اخر
There Other Thing Besids That
بجانب ذلك صدقونى
Beleive in my Words
سوف اعطيك مثال لذلك
I will give probable For you
ان تملك سياره، اعمل
If you own the Car, Do That As
ذلك كما افعل ذلك، انا
Will Say to you, DO That
اعمل ذلك احسن بالعكس
Vacuum yours Car
سيارتك وسوقها وذهبا الى
and Drive It and Go Shoping
shoping صفى سيارتك
and park, after cleaning It
ثم تنظيم سيارتك صفى
(your Car) and go to your Shoping
سيارتك واذهب الى سوق
When you finish From your shoping
وعند انتهاء من سوقى ارجع
Drive your Car to your Home
وسوق سيارتك الى المنزلك
and park you Car When you
وصفى سيارتك، عندما تاتى
Come Second Day to Drive
يوم الثانى كى تسوق سيارتك
your Car and you open your
وتفتح
Car door and you Will
باب سيارتك
Sea Mass of dirt from
وتجد
Where come From?
اين اتت هذه الواحده
is you When you Return
قذاره انت عنيه
From you Shoping
رجعت من سوقى
you drove your Car
وسقه سيارتك

God Creat the Human
Rip
Branch is Eve
Adam the Tree the mother
Earth
حواء ضعف
الارض

continue pag 14
تكمله صفحه 14

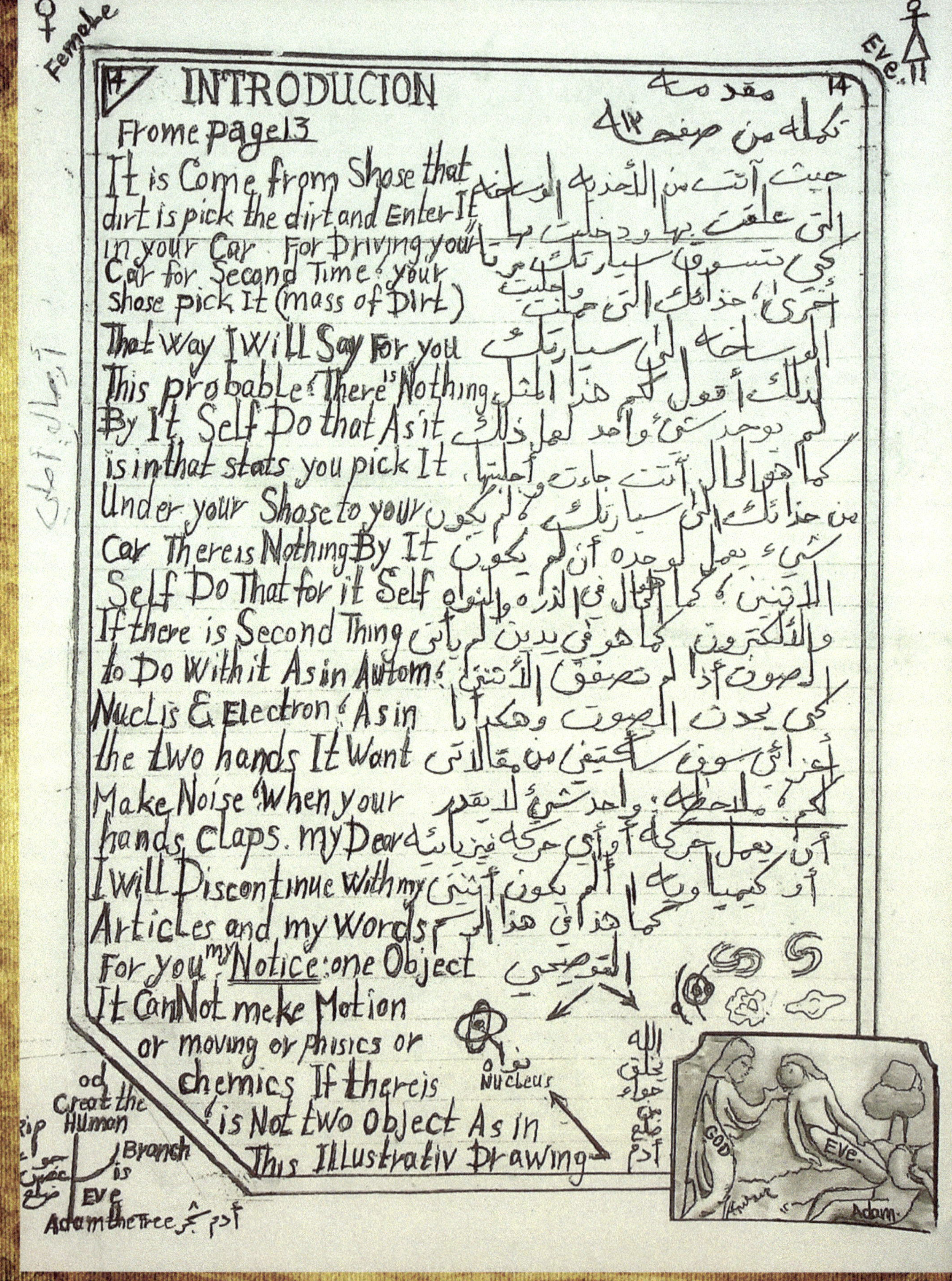

INTRODUCION

Frome page13

It is Come from Shose that
dirt is pick the dirt and Enter It
in your Car   For Driving your
Car for Second Time your
Shose pick It (mass of Dirt)

That Way I will Say For you
This probable There is Nothing
By It Self Do that As it
is in that stats you pick It
Under your Shose to your
Car There is Nothing By It
Self Do That for it Self
If there is Second Thing
to Do With it As in Autom
Nuclis & Electron As in
the two hands It Want
Make Noise When your
hands claps. my Dear
I will Discontinue With my
Articles and my Words
For you my Notice: one Object
It CanNot meke Motion
    or moving or Phisics or
    chemics If there is
    is Not two Object As in
    This Illustrativ Drawing

Nucleus

od the
Creat the
Human
Branch
is
Eve
Adam the tree

Femal
EVE
15
EVE is one of Rip of Adam and part his BODY.
EVE
Eve; is Different As the flower in the fiels Among them. J.E.B.
God Creat the Human
Adam
Branch is Eve.
Earth
Tree is man.
MALE
FEMALE
FEMALE
Branch is Woman.
EVE
WOMAN
MALE
MAN
ADAM
JAB'NEEL
MUD
EARTH
EVE
Look For This picture ((Tree)) Man is Trunk of Tree
And Woman is branch of the tree.
Joseph. E.BahriBek Sun-21-2023
Woman

Female
Eve.
16
Our Roll of Honor
Pertaining all the
Signatures to the "Declaration of Sentiments"
Set forth by the First
Woman's Rights Convention,
held at
Seneca Falls, New York
July 19·20, 1848
LADIES:
Sophronia Taylor
Cynthia Davis
Plant
Lucretia Mott
Harriet Cady Eaton
Margaret Pryor
Elizabeth Ca
Eunice New
Mary Ann
Margaret
Martha
Jane C.
Amy Po
Catheri
Mary A
Lydia
Delia Ma
Catherine
Elizabeth
Malvina Se
PhebeMash
Cathecice Sh
Deborah Scott
Sarah Hallowell
Mary M'Clintock
Mary Gilbert
Rachel D. Bonhel
Betsey Tewksbury
Rhoda Palmer
Margaret Jenkins
Cynthia Fuller
Mary Martin
P. A. Culvert
Susan R. Doty
Rebecca Race
Sarah A. Mosher
Mary E. Vail
Lucy Spalding
Lovina Latham
Sarah Smith
Eliza Martin
Maria E. Wilbur
Elizabeth D. Smith
Caroline Barker
Ann Porter
Experience Gibbs
Antoinette E. Segur
Hannah J. Latham
Sarah Sissoh
Nathan J. Milliken
S. E. Woodworth
Edward F. Underhill
George W. Pryor
Joel Bunker
Isacc VanTassel
Thomas Dell
W. Capron
Richard P. Hunt
Sainval D. Tillm
Justin William
Elika Foote
Fredericke
Henry
Davis
I Love the womans Rights
J*E*B
God Blessed ALL Womens the flowers of the Earth
J.E.B.
Woman should be Equal to man.
J*E*B*
God Creat the Human
RIP
Branch is
Eve
Adam the Tree
Earth
← the mother
God
Eve
Adam

17

Tue * July * 25 * 2023
God Bless All
Woman
Amen

In the Name E.
the Father and
Son and "Holy Spirit.
Amen
My Dears and
My Loves; I ALL-
Way Asak my
mighty Lord
United Us and We
Can't Let Deivl
our Wakenss and Give
him Any Chance to
Let him
Enter Among Us. Amen

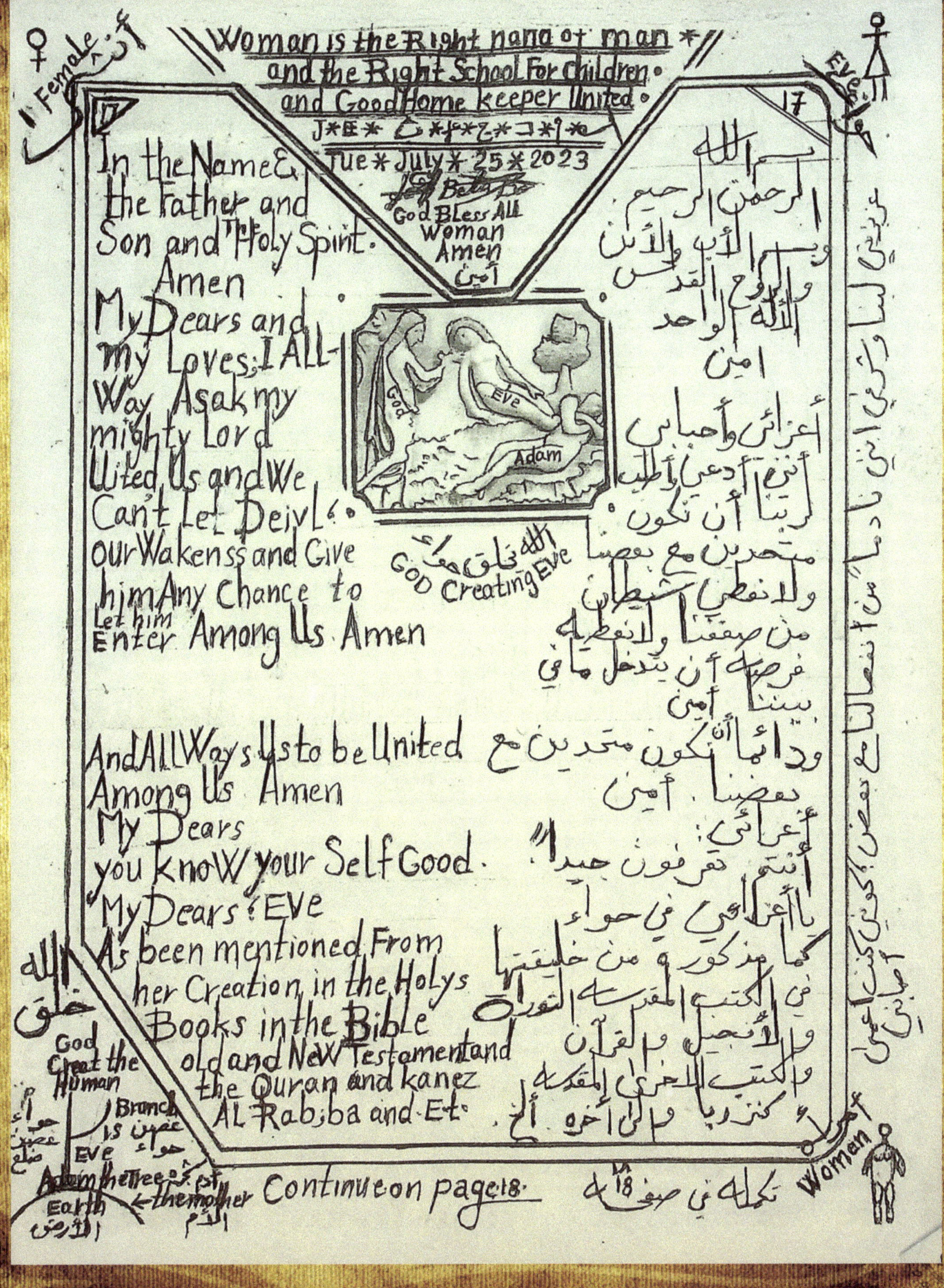

And All Ways Us to be United
Among Us Amen
My Dears
you Know your Self Good.
My Dears ? EVE
As been mentioned From
her Creation in the Holys
Books in the Bible
old and New Testament and
the Quran and kanez
AL Rab;ba and Et.

Continue on page 18.

Woman

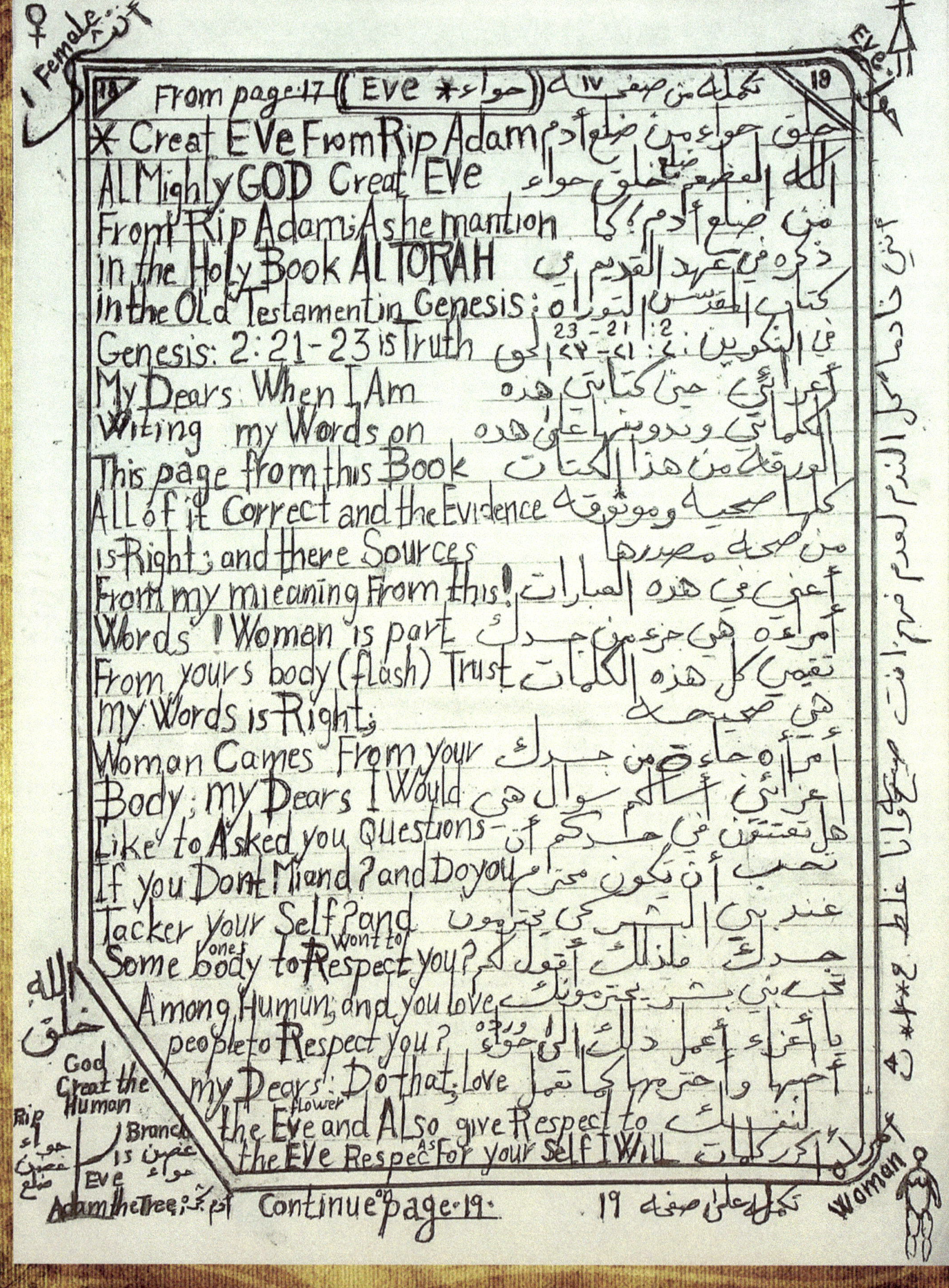
Female
EVE
18 From page 17 (Eve حواء) IV 19
* Creat EVE From Rip Adam
AL Mighly GOD Creat EVE
From Rip Adam: As he mantion
in the Holy Book ALTORAH
in the Old Testament in Genesis:
Genesis: 2: 21-23 is Truth
My Dears When I Am
Witing my Words on
This page from this Book
ALL of it Correct and the Evidence
is Right; and there Sources
From my mieaning From this!
Words ! Woman is part
From yours body (flash) Trust
my Words is Right;
Woman Cames From your
Body; my Dears I Would
Like to Asked you Questions—
If you Dont Miand? and Do you
Tacker your Self? and
Some body to Respect you?
(one)   (wont to)
Among Humun and you love
people to Respect you?
my Dears: Do that, love
the Eve and ALso give Respect to
the EVE Respec For your Self I Will
God Creat the Human
Rip
Eve
Adam the Tree
Continue page 19.
Woman

J*E ※ *J*Z J*9*

Tue * July * 25 * 2023

God Bless All
Woman
Amen

From page 18

Repeat my Words
For you;
My Dears GOD.
Creat Eve. From
his Rip Adam (bone)
he Wants be
Alone him Self
and No be Lonely
By him Self
my Dears; GOD
Did not Creat Eve
to be Merch With
Adam For There plesure;
and Not to be Boring By him Selfs
Along; Offspring of Adam
As I Siad and I Will
Repeated to you Love the Eve
As you Love your Self and Respect.
Not for your Benefits
1- For Yurs pleasure
For your personality
you know What I !! !
mean For you
2- Not to Serve you
she is not Slave As you Think

God
Creat the
Human

Rip

Eve

Adam the tree
Earth

the mother

Continue on page 20.

Female

Eve

Woman

29
20

Tue * July * 25 * 2023

God Bless All
Woman
Amen

From page 19

She is Just As
part of You,
and She is Not
Aliens; From you, she is
Genetically Earthly
From your genetic
Adam.
Meaning of Adam.
I write in my
Book I published
What the Name in the
Bible Means; you
Will See it in Amazon
Post it.
Adam: Earthly + Blood + + م د +
the Spirit of the Lord;
the LORD; he brethed life giving breth into his nostrils
he become Adam life and
Living.

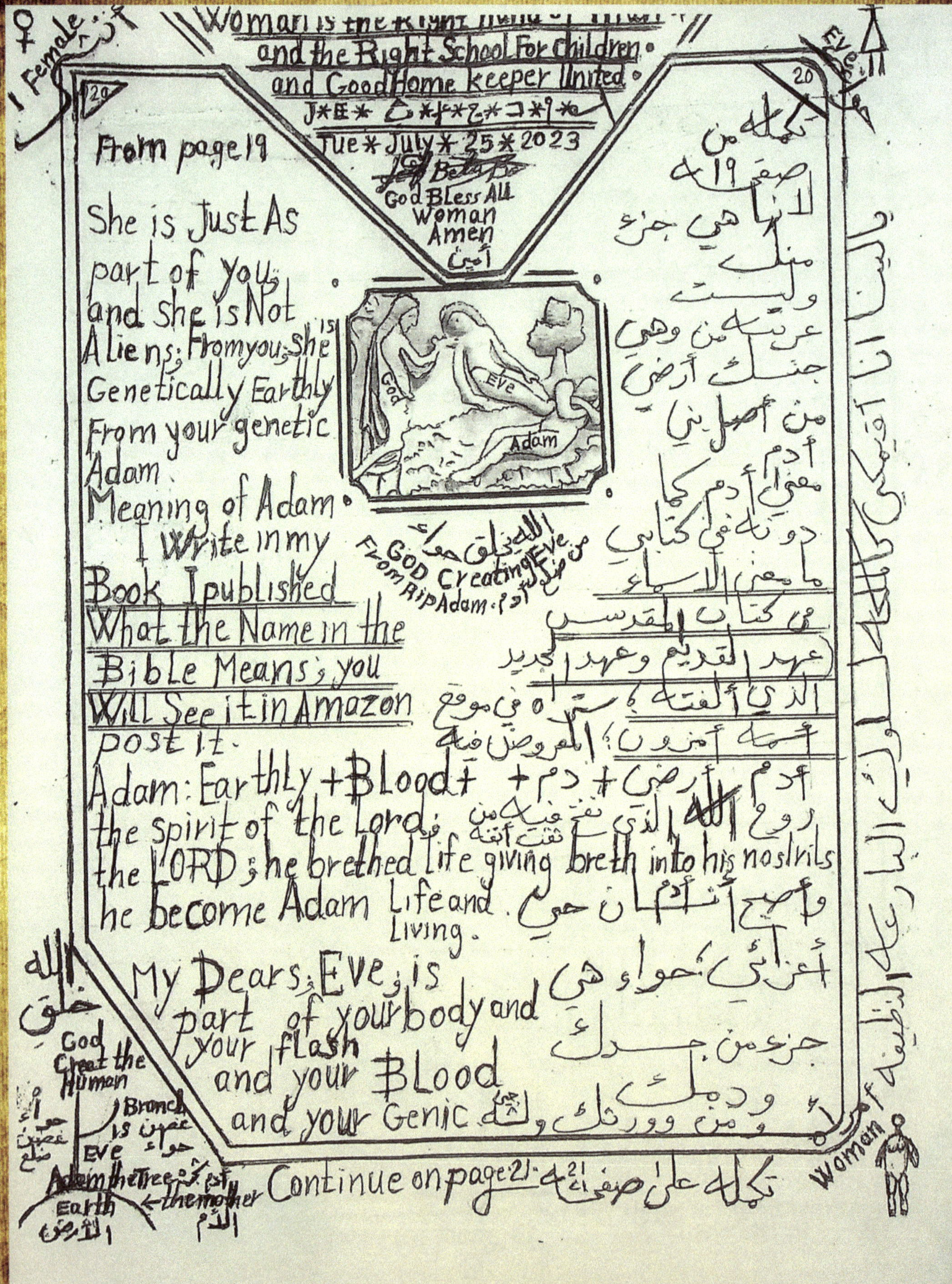

My Dears, Eve, is
part of your body and
your flash
and your Blood
and your Genic

God
Creat the
Human
Branch
is tree
Eve
Adam the tree
← the mother
Earth

Continue on page 21.

Woman

I Female

Eve

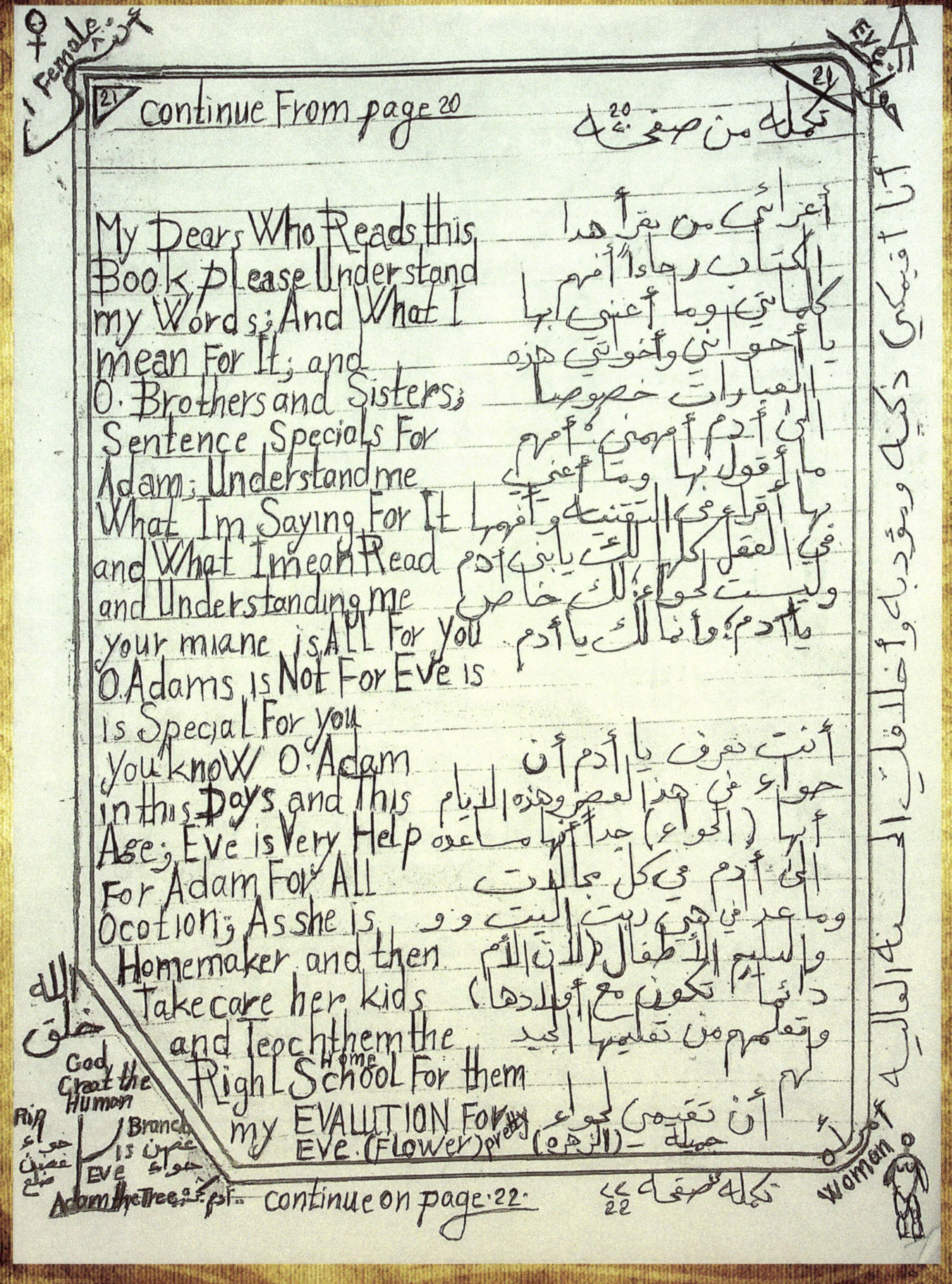

My Dears Who Reads this
Book, Please Understand
my Words; And What I
mean For It; and
O. Brothers and Sisters;
Sentence, Specials For
Adam; Understand me
What I'm Saying For It
and What I mean Read
and Understanding me
your miane is ALL For you
O.Adams is Not For Eve is
is Special For you
you know O. Adam
in this Days and This
Age; Eve is Very Help
For Adam For ALL
Ocotion; As she is
Homemaker, and then
Take care her kids
and Teach them the
Right School For them
my EVALUTION For
Eve. (Flower) pretty

continue on page 22.

J*E* ☾ ☉*✦*2*⅃*9

Tue * July * 25 * 2023

God Bless All
Woman
Amen
أمين

أين تقسمي
حواء فهو
وكلماتي ومقالي
وأقول :-

My Evalution
For the Eve
is and and Words
and my Articals.
I Will Say :-
Eve the Right
hand For Adam
it is Truth
From this
Articals it is
Rights, and
their is Other
Articals; As they
Saying :-
Behind the Great man a
Woman; this Expression
I Agree From Source is is
Right Comes
This ALL my Articales For you
is Right

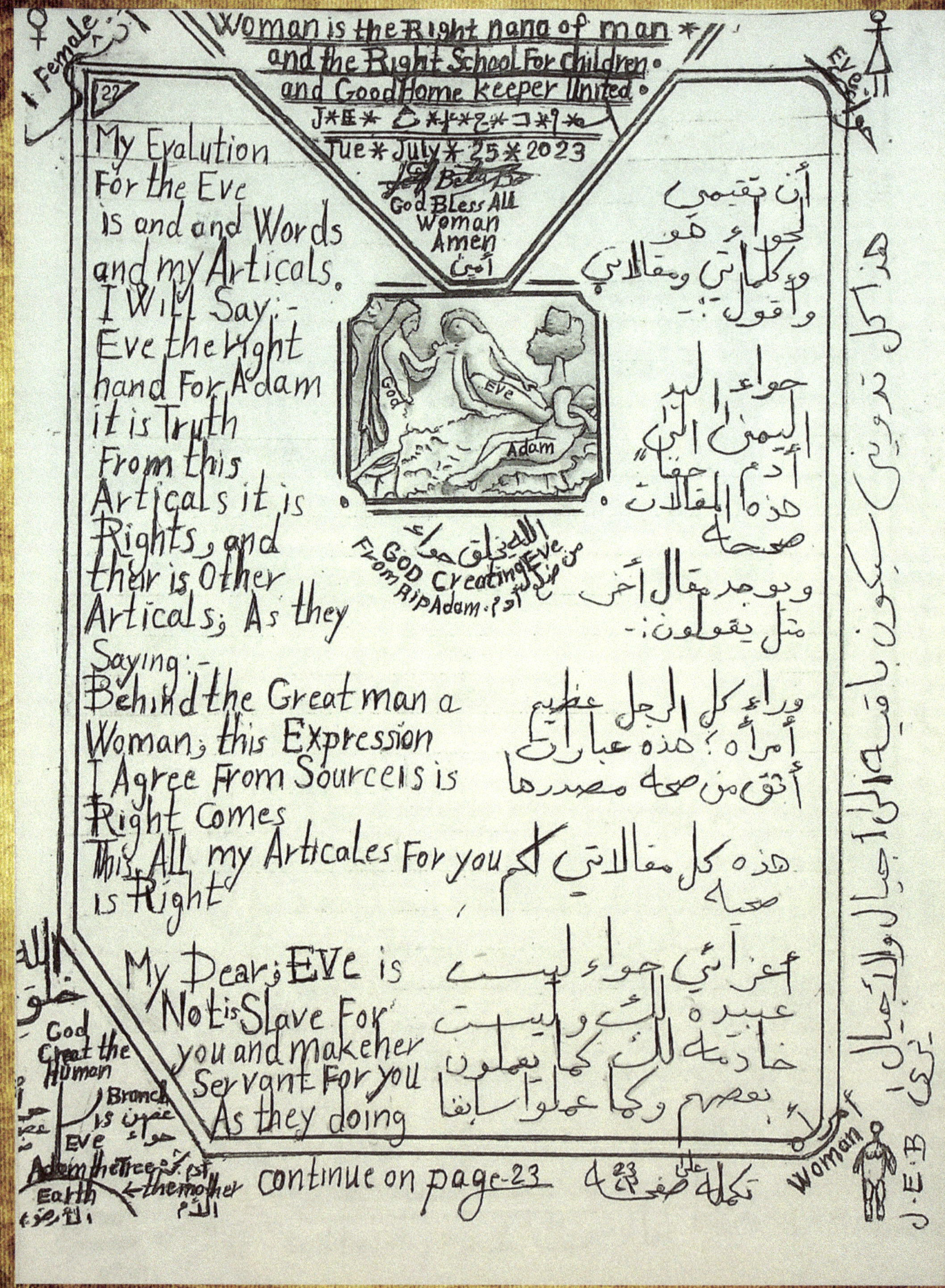

حواء اليد
اليمنى التي
آدم هذا
هذا المقالات
صحه
ويوجد مقال أخر
مثل يقولون :-

وراء كل رجل عظيم
أمرأه؟ هذه عبارات
أتفق من صحه مصدرها
هذه كل مقالاتي لكم
صحه

عزائي حواء ليست
عبده لك وليست
خادمة لك كما يفعلون
بعضهم وكما فعلوا آنفا

My Dear; EVE is
Not is Slave For
you and make her
Servant For you
As they doing

God
Creat the
Human
Branch
is tree
Eve
Adam the tree
Earth ← the mother

continue on page-23

تكملة على صفحة 23

Woman

J.E.B

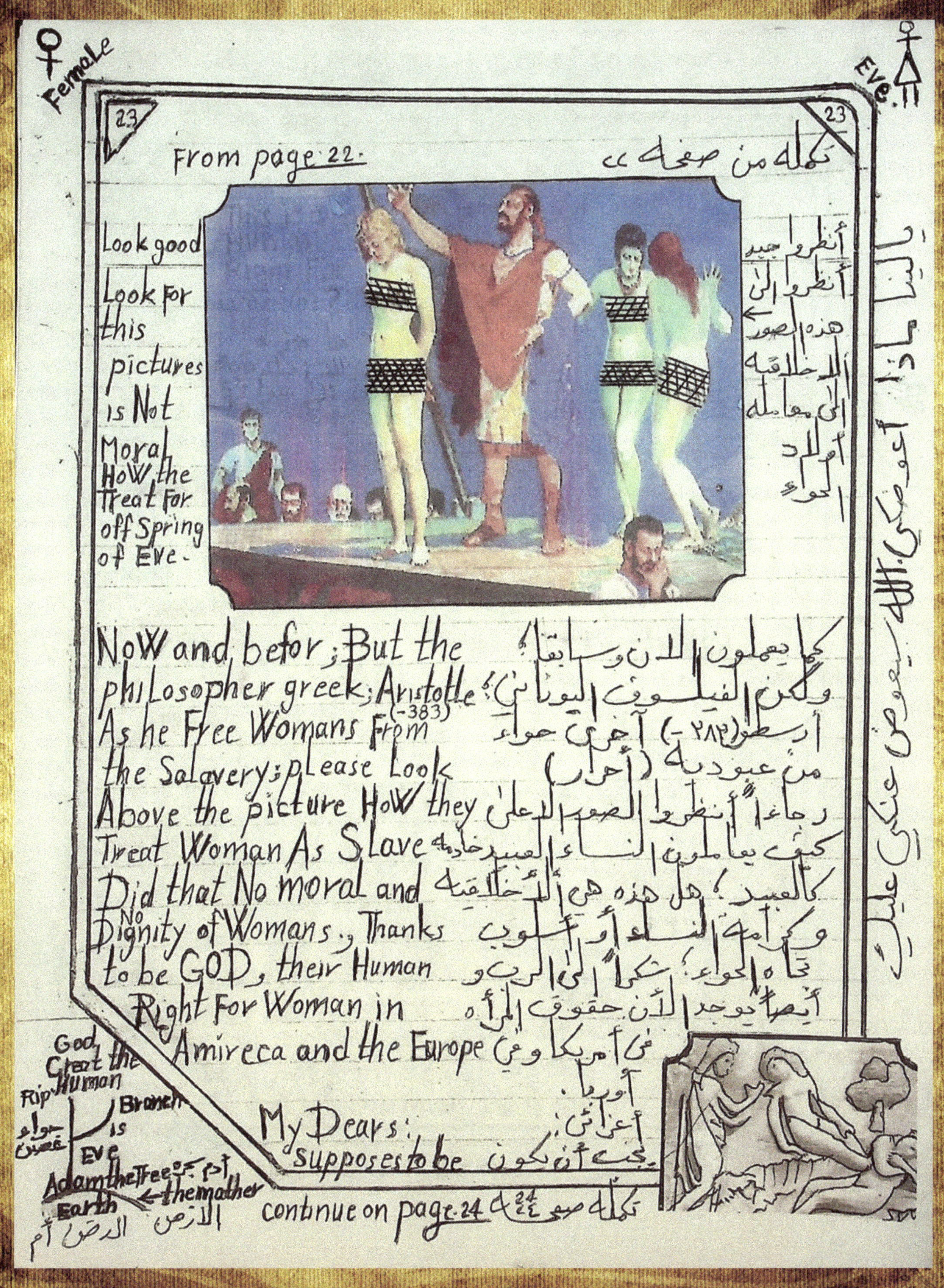

continue on page. 24

Woman is the Right hand of man and the Right School For children. and Good Home keeper United.

Tue * July * 25 * 2023

God Bless All Woman Amen

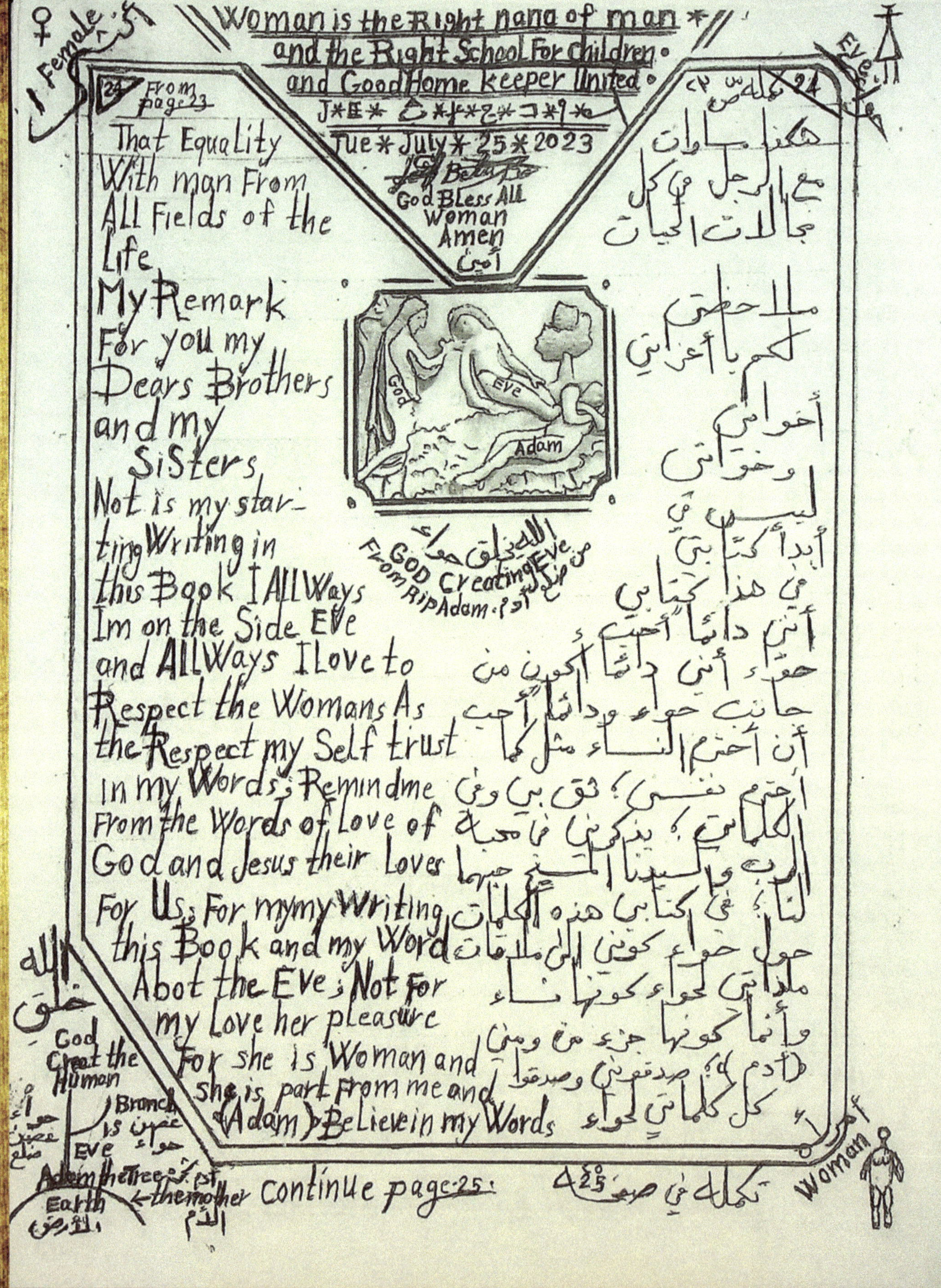

From page 23

That Equality With man From All Fields of the Life My Remark For you my Dears Brothers and my Sisters. Not is my starting Writing in this Book I AllWays Im on the Side Eve and AllWays I Love to Respect the Womans As the Respect my Self trust in my Words, Remind me From the Words of Love of God and Jesus their Lover For Us, For my my Writing this Book and my Word Abot the Eve, Not For my Love her pleasure For she is Woman and she is part From me and (Adam) Believe in my Words

Continue page 25.

هكذا باقى عمل مع الرجل فى كل مجالات الحياة
ملاحظتى لكم يا اعزائى اخوانى وخواتى
ليس ابداً كتابتى فى هذا الكتاب انتم دائماً احب
انى دائماً اكون من جانب حواء ودائماً احب
ان احترم النساء مثل ما احترم نفسى؟ ثق بى فى
الكلمات يذكرنى ما حبه واعيسنا المسيح حبه
لنا، فى كتابى هذا الكلمات حول حواء كونى الى ملاحظات
ملادتى حواء كونها انا وانا كونها جزء منى ومن
آدم؟ صدقونى وصدقوا كل كلماتى حواء

تكلمك فى صفحة ٢٥

J*E* ☾ *۴*۲*コ*۹*

From Page 24

Tue * July * 25 * 2023

God Bless All Woman. Amen
آمين

For Eve.
my Dears: Sisters
and my Brothers
God creat Eve
pretty Among,
and Different
Among them All
of them they Are
prettys and you
cannot Say Some
Eve they Not prettys
you cannot Say That. or
your Opinin or your Mood to
Judge she is Not pretty in Some
man, Opinin Love the One you
Not choose he Will choose her
in his Heart and then she
Will be the Love one For him
the pretty flower one Amen

* J*E*B* *コ*۱*۲* *

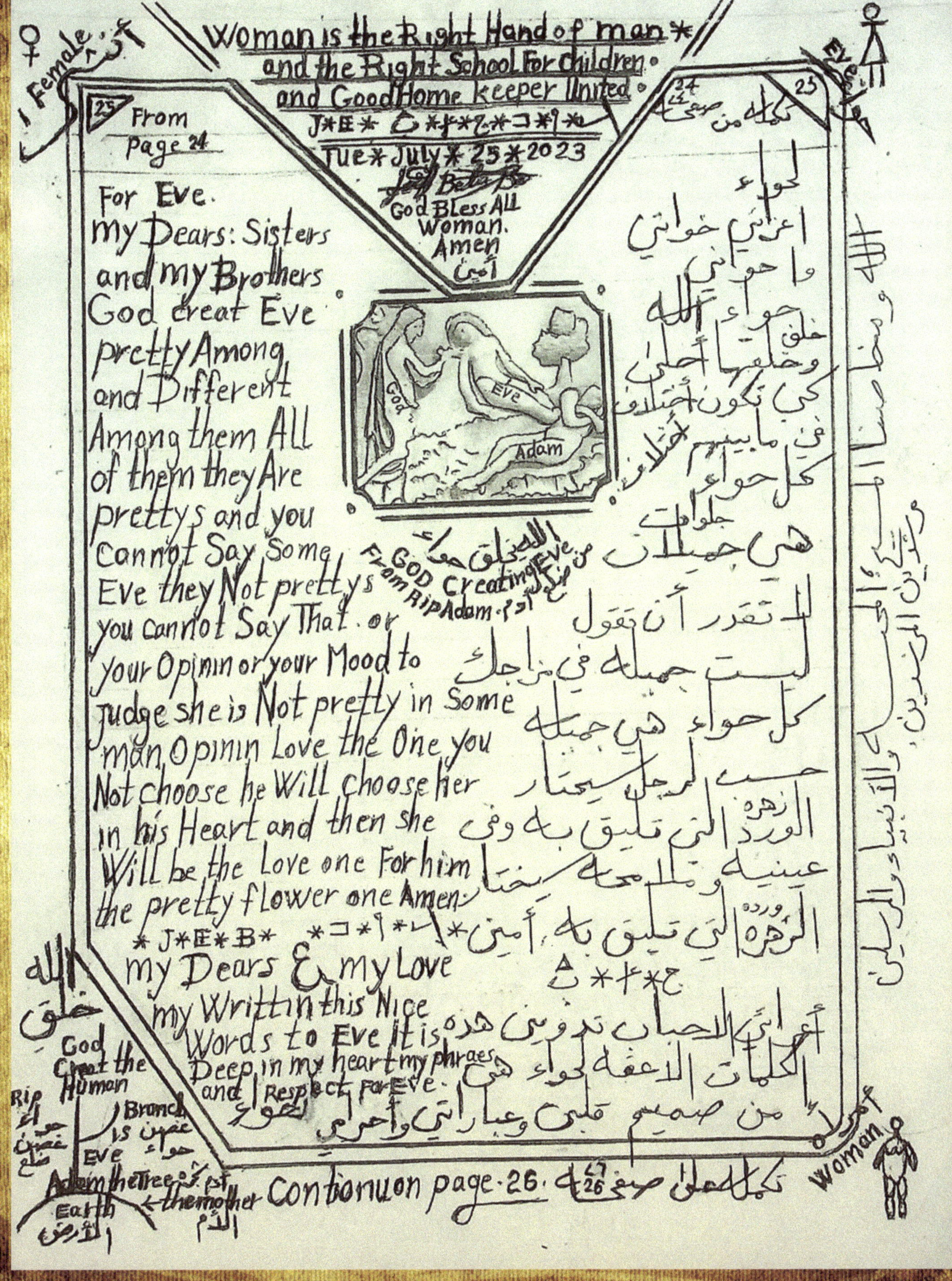

my Dears & my Love
my Writtin this Nice
Words to Eve it is
Deep in my heart my phraes.
and I Respect ForEve.

God
Creat the
Human
Rip
Branch
is
Eve
Adam the tree
← the mother
Earth

Contionu on page. 26.

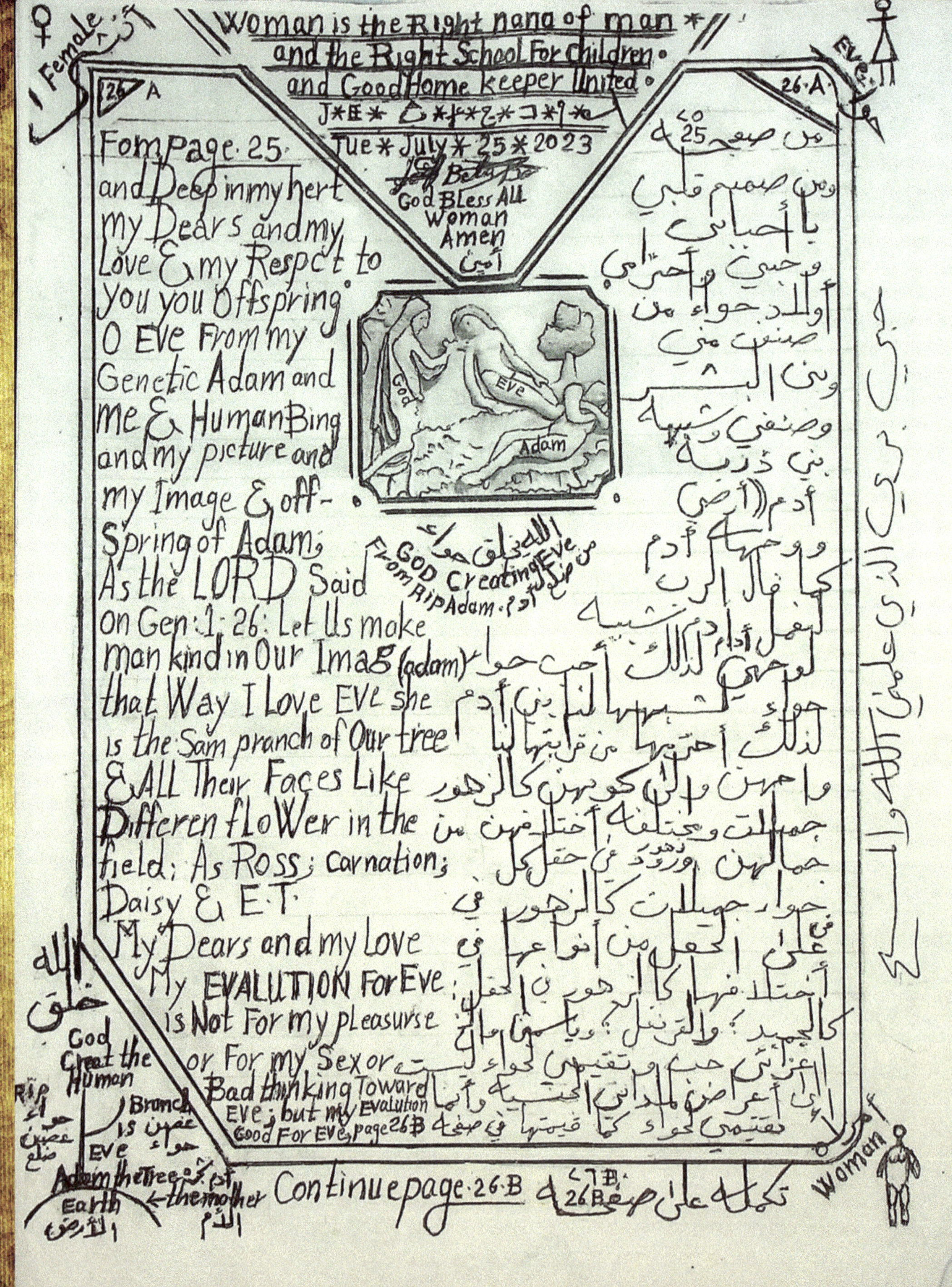

Fom Page. 25.
and Deep in my hert
my Dears and my
Love & my Respct to
you you Offspring
O Eve From my
Genetic Adam and
me & Human Bing
and my picture and
my Image & off-
Spring of Adam,
As the LORD Said
on Gen: 1: 26: Let Us moke
man kind in Our Imag (adam)
that Way I Love Eve she
is the Sam pranch of Our tree
& ALL Their Faces Like
Differen floWer in the
field; As Ross; carnation;
Daisy & E.T.
My Dears and my Love
My EVALUTION For Eve
is Not For my pleasurse
or For my Sex or
Bad thinking Toward
Eve; but my Evalution
Good For Eve, page 26 B

Continue page. 26 B

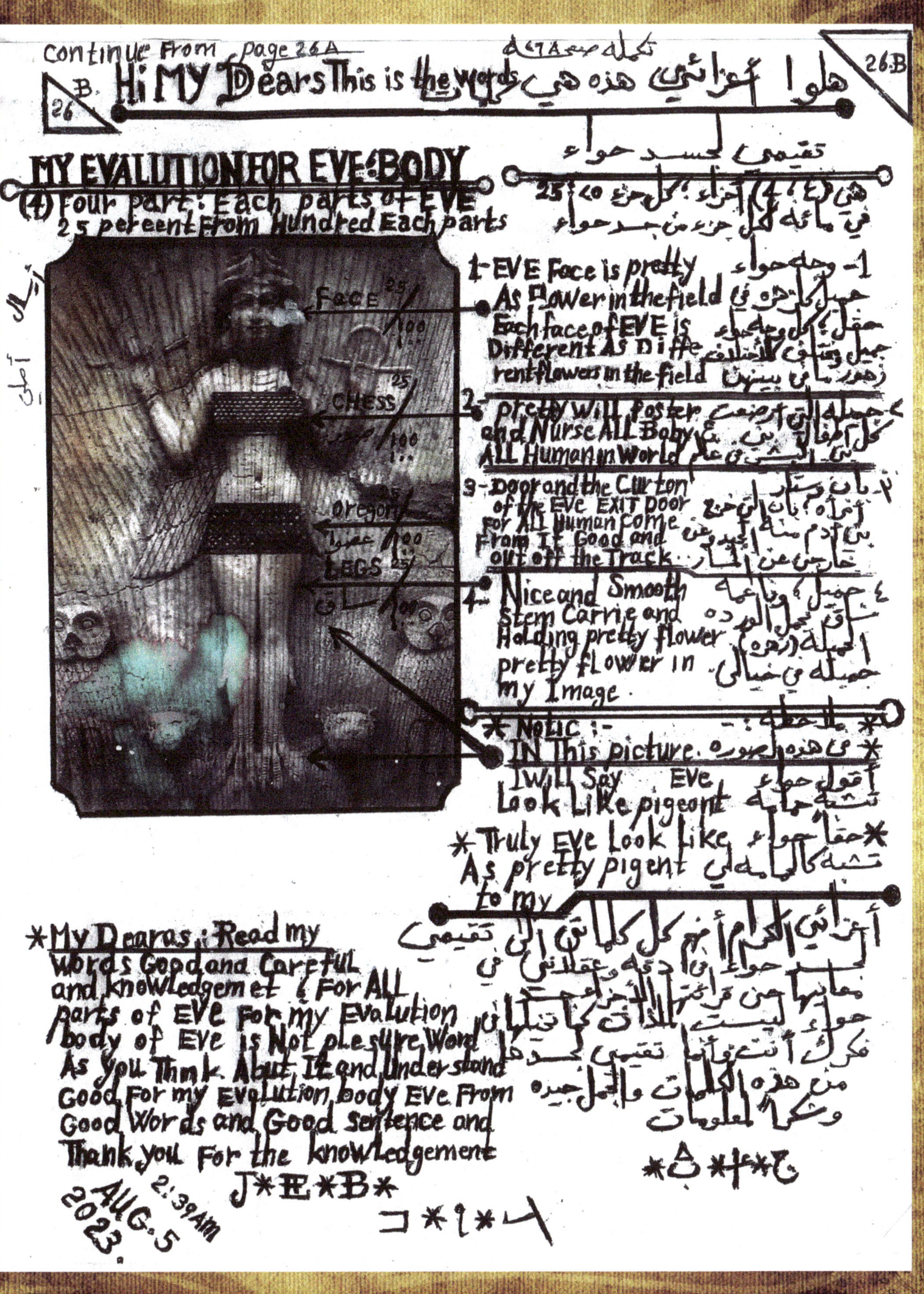

continue From page 26A
26 B.   Hi MY Dears This is the words
هلو! أعزائي هذه هي كلمات

26.B

MY EVALUTION FOR EVE-BODY
(4) Four part: Each parts of EVE
25 percent From Hundred Each parts
تقسيم لجسد حواء

1- EVE Face is pretty
As Flower in the field
Each face of EVE is
Different As Diffe
rent flowers in the field

FACE 25/100

2- pretty will Foster
and Nurse ALL Boby
ALL Human in World

CHESS 25/100

3- Door and the Curton
of the EVE EXIT Door
for All Human come
From It Good and
out off the Track

oregon 25/100
LEGS 25/100

4- Nice and Smooth
Stem Carrie and
Holding pretty flower
pretty flower in
my Image

* Nolic :-
IN This picture.
I will Say   EVE
Look Like pigeont

* Truly EVE Look Like
As pretty pigent
to my

* My Dearas : Read my
words Good and Careful
and knowledgemet (For ALL
parts of EVE For my Evalution
body of EVE is Not plesure Word
As You Think About It and Understand
Good For my Evolution, body EVE From
Good Words and Good sentence and
Thank you For the knowledgement
J*E*B*
2:39AM
AUG-5
2023.

Continue Page 28

continue page 29

Female
Eve
Woman is the Right Hand of man.
and the Right School For children.
and Good Home keeper United.
Tue * July * 25 * 2023
God Bless All woman Amen
God
Eve
Adam
GOD Creating Eve From Rip Adam
God Creat the Human
Branch is Eve
Adam the tree
the mother
Earth
Continue pag 30
Woman

Woman is the Right Hand of man
and the Right School For children
and Good Home keeper United
Tue * July * 25 * 2023
God Bless All
Woman
Amen
Female
Eve
30
30
29
29
God
Eve
Adam
GOD Creating Eve
From RipAdam
God Creat the Human
Branch is Eve
Adam the tree
the mother
Earth
God Bless
Woman

Woman is the Right Hand of man
and the Right School For Children
and Good Home keeper United
Tue * July * 25 * 2023
God Bless All woman Amen
God
Eve
Adam
God Creating Eve From Rip Adam?
Female
Eve
God Creat the Human
Branch
Eve
Adam the tree
Earth
the mother
31
31
MON. AUG. 21. 2023
10:00pm
Woman

the End

My Dears Valuedone
I Admire for GOD Creation
For All Think in Vast Univers
and the Earth Seene Unseen
or micro or Far on in this
Vast Univers and from the
Spiril BLOW inour Body and
the Angels and the Air
All of them have No Colors
Smells and No test
and Any think Turly
his Creatin is Mysterious
As he Creat them, seene
and Unseen, Im Very
Surprise and Im Very
Admire from his
Creation the the Work
I took 6 years For his
Great is Not 6 Days As
Been Mention in the old
testament the Lord
has No Measuremet
Nothing to be Measurse
and Do Whats he
Wants my Dears
GOD Great Diff
erent oregen
For All his

الختام

أعزائي الكرام
أني معجب في خليقة كل
الأشياء الرب خلقها
في هذا الكون الفسيح
وعلى الأرض يرى وما
لا يرى مجهرية أو بعيدة
في هذا الكون الفسيح
ومن أيضاً الروح الذي
نفخ بنا والملائكة والهواء
كلهم ليست لها اللون ورائحة
ولا طعم ولا أي شيء
حقاً خليقته أنها غامضة
الذي عملها الأشياء يرى
وما لا يرى أنني جداً مدهش
ومعجب من خليقة عمله التي
استغرقت 6 الألف لخليقة
وليست *6 أيام كما مدونة في
كتاب المقدس العهد القديم
الرب لا يملك أي مقاييس
وأي شيء لقياس وعمل الذي
يريده
أعزائي أنظر بدقة كل أشياء
لها حيات على الأرض
تختلف فيما بينهم في اختلاف
أعضاء في الأشياء الذي خلقها
كالبني البشر وعصافير وحيوانات

* يوم عند الله هو 1000 الف سنة
* يوم واحد = 1000 سنة عند ربنا

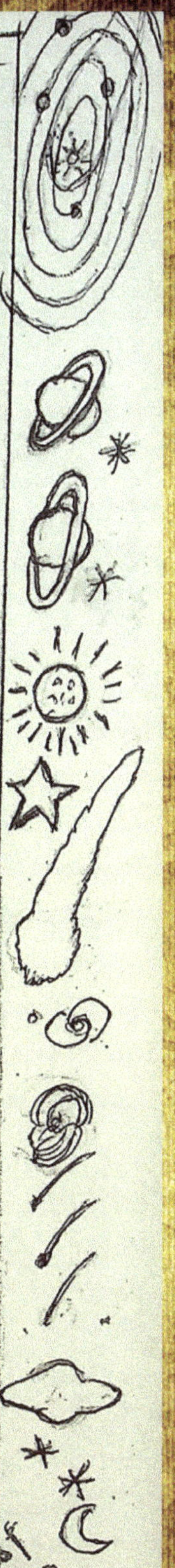

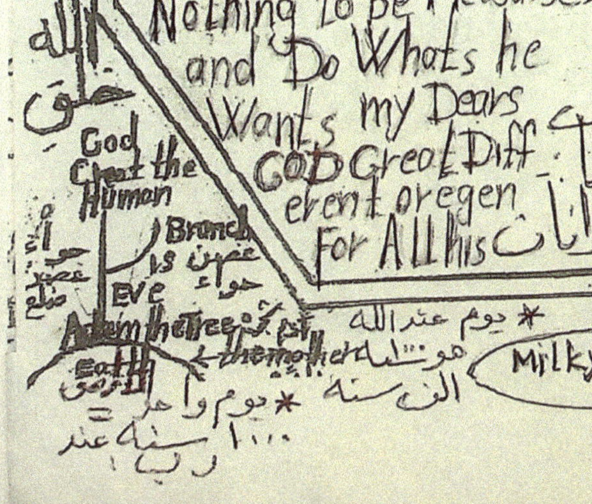

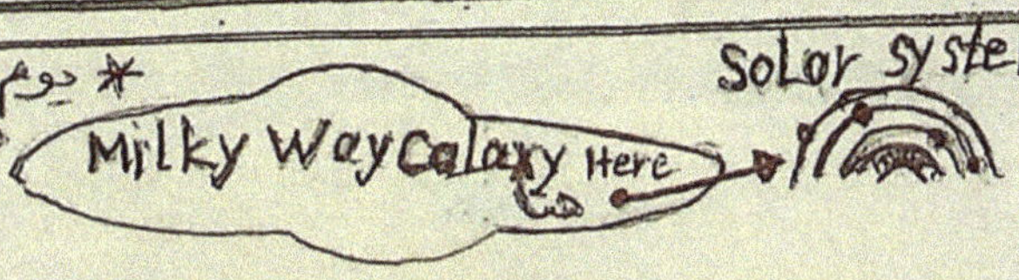

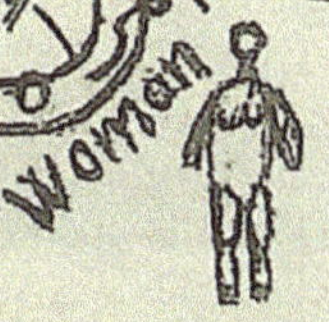

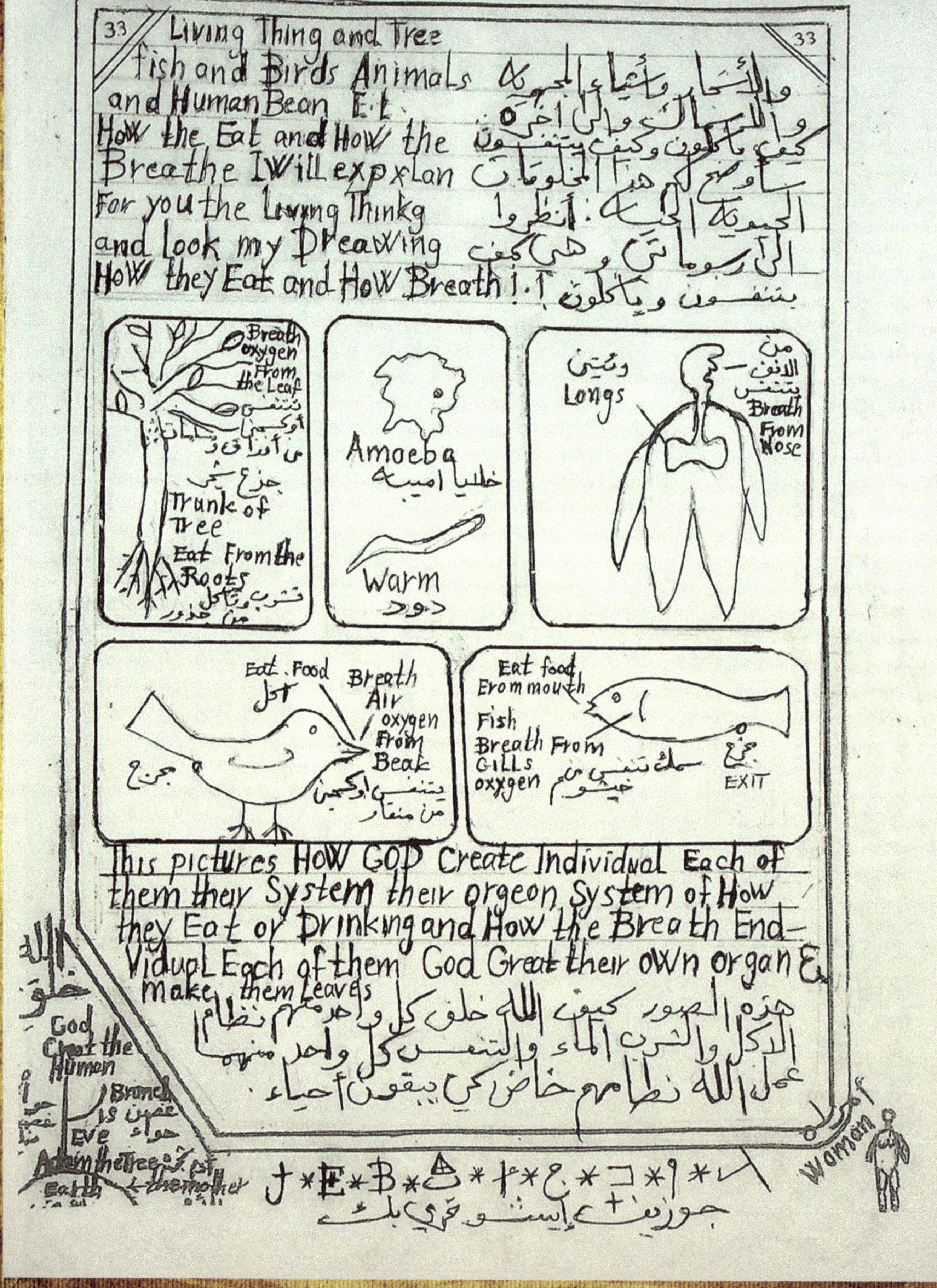
33   Living Thing and Tree

fish and Birds Animals &
and Human Bean E.t
How the Eat and How the
Breathe I Will explan
For you the Living Thinkg
and look my Dreawing
How they Eat and How Breath i.t

33

Breath oxygen From the Leaf
Trunk of Tree
Eat From the Roots

Amoeba

Warm

Longs
Breath From Nose

Eat Food
Breath Air oxygen From Beak

Eat food From mouth
Fish
Breath From GiLLs oxxgen
EXIT

This pictures HOW GOD Create Individual Each of
them their System their orgeon System of How
they Eat or Drinking and How the Breath End-
vidupL Each of them God Great their own organ &
make them Leaves

God Creat the Human
Bronch is the Eve
Adim the tree Eath   the mother

Woman

أخي انطوان وانا مع أهل منزو
Me and my twin Brother Antione
عيد ميلادنا أنا وانطوان
Our Birthday Antione and me 12 years old
* We Are
I Am (Joseph) Sitting at Dining Room at our House at Al Mansor City Bahgdad - IRAQ
في عرفة طعام في بيتنا في مدينة المنصور بغداد عراق
Our Dining Room at our House Al Mansor City - Bahgdad - IRAQ
غرفتنا الطعام في بيتنا في مدينة المنصور

35
٤
قبرص
اول قسمة لجبل كنيسة مديس كوركيس أثينان
At top Mountain at st george church.
ATHEN - Greek
Me*
At
Work with Good and Nice
All worker with me
ع عمال معمل شعل
ع الباء
الطيبين
J*E*B*
*قرأ*ل
*٦٤*ح

My Love
My pretty
My Dear ↑ RAMINA AT EASTER VIGIL ↑
عيوني راميناي كبيرتي في عشقتي دلوعتي
My Sweet heart. ((My Wife))

At Creek — ATHEN on TOP
Mountain at the church
St. George Creek
ATHEN 1976

أنا في أعالي بيتاي ي انقناي
كبنك كسين مرسى ممة 14 الجبل
كور كسين
1947
1976

J*E*B
J*9*J
C**J*2.

Carolin my Sister in Law
and my Doughte Lillian
(my Dears pretty Angel Doughter

عيوني كاترين كارولين اخت زوجتي
عينين ليلي ننتي ع
الحلوى

Creek ATHEN
St. George Church 1976
كور كسين
كنك فقدسني جرجس عة في لبت

My Dear Sister

My Sister   Mariam at Living Room
At AL Mansour city Bahgdad - IRAQ

أختي العزيزه مريم في غرفة الجلوس
من بيتنا في مدينة المنصور بغداد عراق

اختك

Front Door of church -
My Mom and Mother
Um Samy Aunt Zakia
at St. George church. 1976
ATHEN - Creek

أمام حديقتنا أنا أمام شجرتنا النخيل

38
My Angel My Dear Daughter Lillian→ My Sweet heart (Lilly)
عزيزتي إبنتي الحلوه ليلى ليليان
My Mom & Me Greek Athen 1976
My Dear twian Anton at his bed at Al Mansour City
في سبعينات من مدينه منصور بغداد عراق
عمي أخي التوأمان أنطون في غرفه نوم (يوما)
In our Apt.
Im. chicago ILL. 1978
في شكاغو في شقتنا

↑ I Am praying

Ramina in church of
St. gregory church
San Mateo Ca.
at Easte Vigil Night

(أنا مذنب)
الله يبارك لك لفضلك لي
صلّي

في شقتها!
القريبه
وحسيني
العاله
غائبه
عني وأنا
وأنا لوحدي
وليست
عزيزي
معي.
خطوبه
حلوه لبنان
شقاقه
١٩٧٨
أبامنا اللوو قصتنا
بالكمان ذنى
J.E.B.

pretty
Angel
عزيزتي زوجتي رامينا مع أولادي
My Dear wife
Ramina with
My Dears kid
Lillian Jack
& Shamy
Birthy Shamam the cute
Wit her cousin
cute Romy my
Niece my sweet
(pretty) NOR   نور
E*B
(اللوه)
عيد ميلاد اللوه جميلة: مع أبنت العم أنطوان
اللوه أبنتي شيران (Sham & Romy) ودعي اللوه الجميلة

my
Dear
sweet heart
my mom

Me at
our House
Baghdad-IRAQ
ALmansor City
70 s
انا بيتنا
في بغداد-عراق
في مدينة
المنصور انا بسبعينات
Mein 70 s

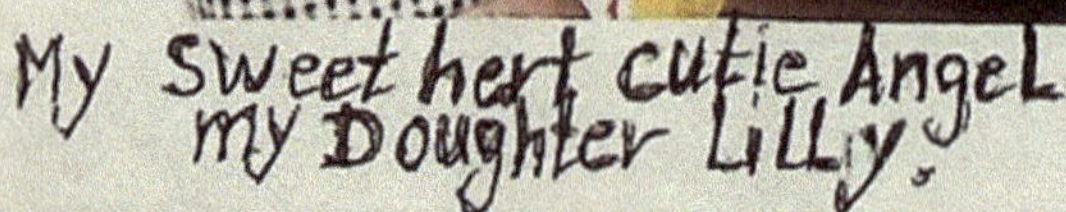
My sweet hert cutie Angel
my Doughter LiLLy

me Holding Space craft
USA Apollo 11 Eagle
انا وحامل في يدي سفينة فضاء مركبة
الفضائية أبولو 11 الأمريكية

in 1978
42 my
Apt. at
In chicago
Foster and
Clark street
I Rented It
For $100°°
a month 1978
my.
Engineering
Drawing
Little Room.
and
my Love!
Image my Love
Dancing
in my
Front Imge my Face
my Face
وخيال جبي
يترقص أمام
وجهي .978
١ من ١١ صفحه مصوره
at chicago
1978
42
أيامي الحلوه
مع جميع وجهي
الي لنا !
عندما كنت
وأنا لوحدي
وابكي جبي
الغاليه وابتبه
الحلوه !
my Bed Room
غرفتي النوم
شقتنا أنا واطوان ولبوي شيكاغو 1979
our Apt. me. Atiotnand leo
((my Brothers))

43
43
J *E *B
THE LIF ONLY EXIST ON THE EARTH
and
GOD CREAT EVE FROM RIP ADAM
THE RIGHT ADAM English and Arabic
EVE
MON - AUG - 21 2023 office 12:06Am

44
44

My Dears As I Saind Befor; EVe the
Right Hand of Adam you can See EVE
in All field Look this Book Below, I
Bough it from Library, the Good Book About
Eve; Share Adam For All field. J.E.B

أعزائي كما قلت سابقاً حول السـ
الـ أعزائي إذا نظرت إلى الكتاب
الذي اشتريته من مكتبة كتاب
حواء تشارك أدم في كل المجالات .ب.ح.ج

This Book is posted Above is GoodBook. هذا الكتاب في أعلى أنه جيد.

My Dears If you sea in this Book Below about Lot of Woman Side By Side of Adom, you Will Seathem in the All field of the life and they Work As man inALL Brunchs, If you Look Copon the Names of Womans inALL science field

أعوانى أذا رأيت فى هذا الكتاب جيد حول كثير من النساء جانبى الى جانب أدم ستراهن فى جميع مالات الحياة وأنهن حد واهمن ويعملون كالرجال فى كل فروع أذا نظرت فى هذا القسمه واماتهن فى كل جالات العلوم

CHIEN-SHIUNG WU (1912—1997)
HEDY LAMARR (1914—2000)
MAMIE PHIPPS CLARK (1917—1983)
GERTRUDE ELION (1918—1999)
KATHERINE JOHNSON (1918—)
JANE COOKE WRIGHT (1919—2015)
ROSALIND FRANKLIN (1920—1958)
ROSALYN YALOW (1921—2011)
ESTHER LEDERBERG (1922—2006)
STATISTICS IN STEM
VERA RUBIN (1928—2016)
ANNIE EASLEY (1933—2011)
JANE GOODALL (1934—)
SYLVIA EARLE (1935—)
VALENTINA TERESHKOVA (1937—)
PATRICIA BATH (1942—)
CHRISTIANE NÜSSLEIN-VOLHARD (19..
JOCELYN BELL BURNELL (1943—)
SAU LAN WU (1947—)
ELIZABETH BLACKBURN (1948—)
KATIA KRAFFT (1942—1991)
MAE JEMISON (1956—)
MAY-BRITT MOSER (1963—)
MARYAM MIRZAKHANI (1977—2017)

INTRODUCTION
HYPATIA (350-370CE— 415CE [?])
MARIA SIBYLLA MERIAN (1647—1717)
WANG ZHENYI (1768—1797)
MARY ANNING (1799—1847)
ADA LOVELACE (1815—1852)
ELIZABETH BLACKWELL (1821—1910)
HERTHA AYRTON (1854—1923)
KAREN HORNEY (1885—1952)
NETTIE STEVENS (1861—1912)
FLORENCE BASCOM (1862—1945)
MARIE CURIE (1867—1934)
MARY AGNES CHASE (1869—1963)
TIMELINE
LISE MEITNER (1878—1968)
LILLIAN GILBRETH (1878—1972)
EMMY NOETHER (1882—1955)
EDITH CLARKE (1883—1959)
MARJORY STONEMAN DOUGLAS (1890—1..
ALICE BALL (1892—1916)
GERTY CORI (1896—1957)
JOAN BEAUCHAMP PROCTER (1897—1931)
CECILIA PAYNE-GAPOSCHKIN (1900—19..
BARBARA MCCLINTOCK (1902—1992)
MARIA GOEPPERT-MAYER (1906—1972)
GRACE HOPPER (1906—1992)
RACHEL CARSON (1907—1964)
LAB TOOLS

Woman is the Right Hend of man
and the Right School For Children.
and Good Home keeper United.

J*E* ☐ ⚹ ⚹ ⚹ ⚹

Tue * July * 25 * 2023

God Bless All
Woman
Amen

To End My
Writing.
My Dears, my
Py Describe my
Final Evalution and
to Evaluation of Eve
is As Branch of the
Tree Sprouteb
From Tree It is
As Very fragiel I
Describe her
When the Wind
All Way the Wind is
strong Blow Up the
Branch & Break it Becays
is Weaks How the Eve she
is Weaks; I Decribe the
Eve Weakers then Adam As
Tree you have to be Careful With
Eve and Nice; Dont Not Blow Up
on Eve As the Wind Blow Up on
the Branch of Tree; or As the cat
When you hurt her; she will
Scratch you; Becays you
hurt her; and As the
flower in the pot when
Water it; Which I
mean you have
to Love your Eve
to United with you. J*E*B*

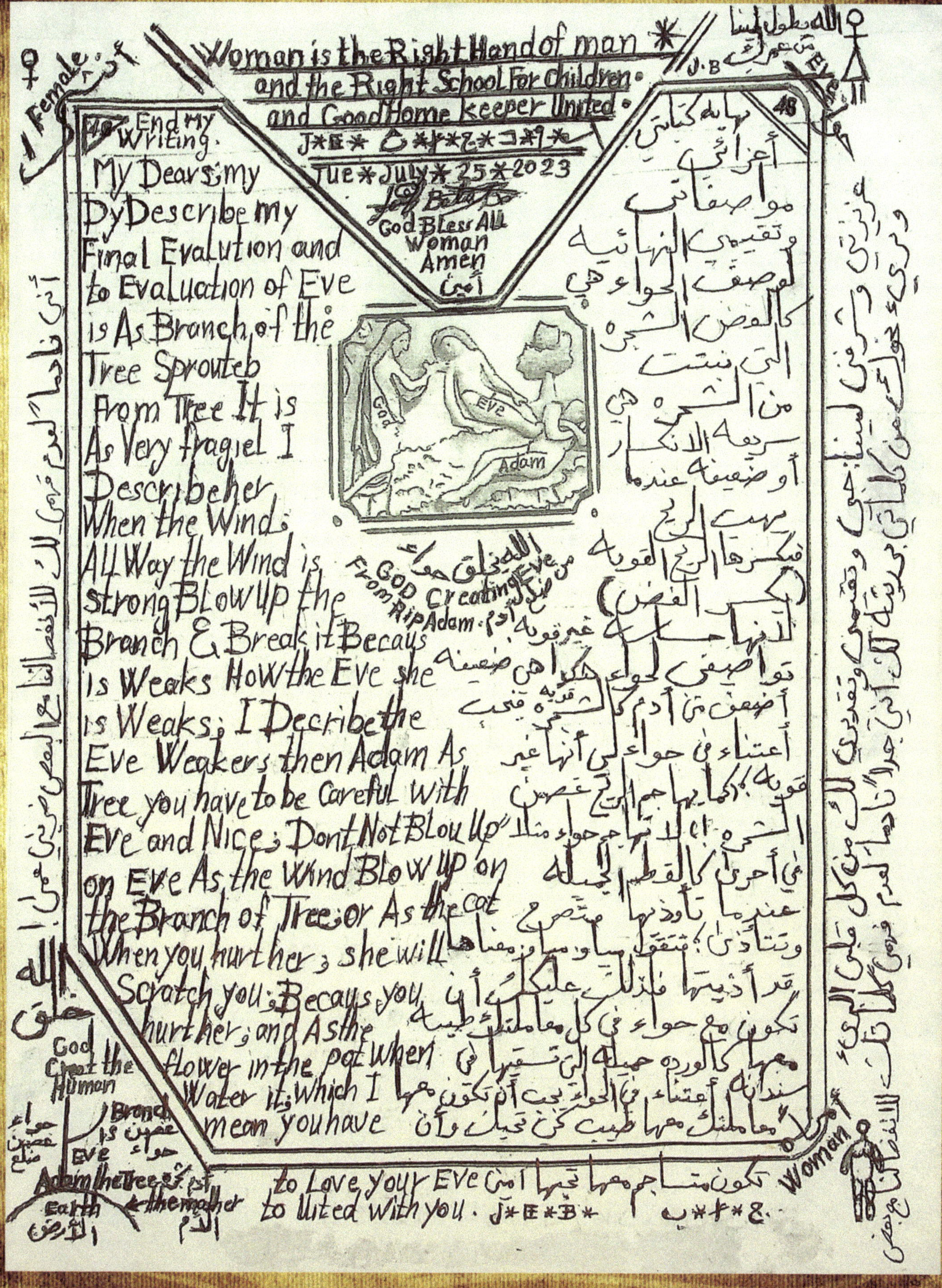

Female

God Creat the
Human

Brand
is
Eve

Adam the tree
Earth & the mother

God

Woman

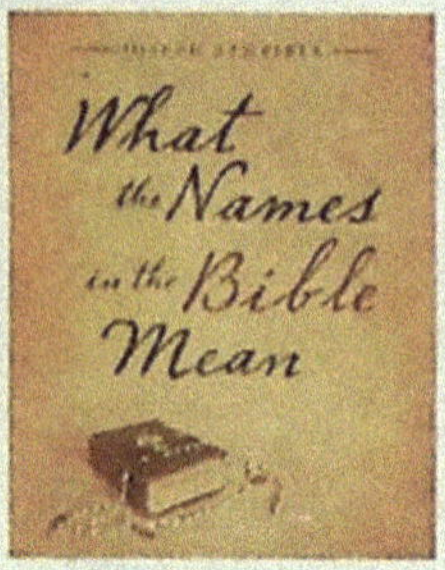

What the Names in the Bible Mean
by Joseph Bahribek | May 20, 2020
★★★★★ 1
Paperback
$17.99
✓prime
FREE delivery Sat, Sep 2 on $25 of items shipped by Amazon
Or fastest delivery Wed, Aug 30
More Buying Choices
$1.39 (17 used & new offers)

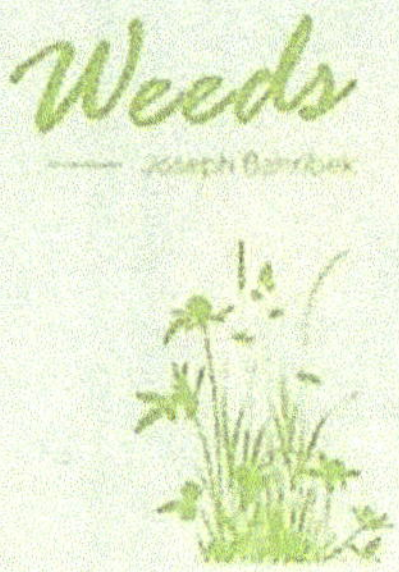

Weeds
by Joseph Bahribek | Aug 19, 2021
Kindle
$3.99 Print List Price: ~~$10.99~~
Available instantly
Paperback
$10.99
✓prime
$5.99 delivery Sat, Sep 2
Only 1 left in stock - order soon.
More Buying Choices
$10.16 (3 new offers)

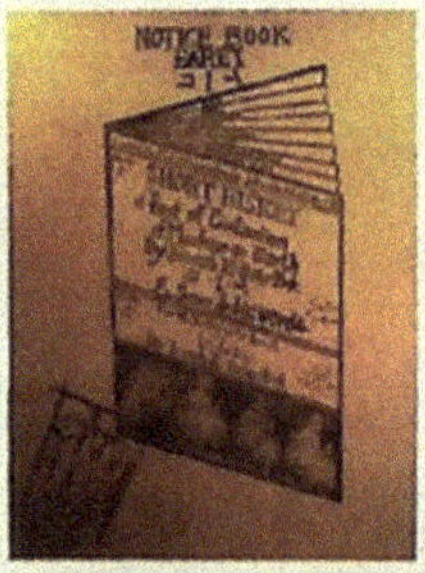

Notice Book: Earey (Arabic Edition)
Arabic Edition | by Joseph E Bahribek | Jun 7, 2023
Paperback
$15.99
✓prime
FREE delivery Sep 5 - 8 on $25 of items shipped by Amazon

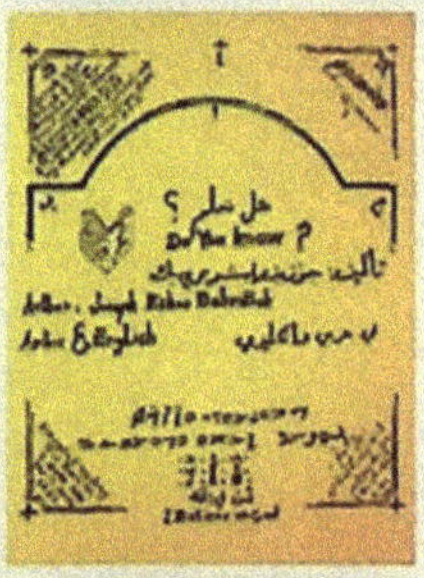

Do You Know (Arabic Edition)
Arabic Edition | by Joseph Eshoo Bahribek | May 16, 2023
Paperback
$26.99
✓prime
FREE delivery Sep 5 - 11

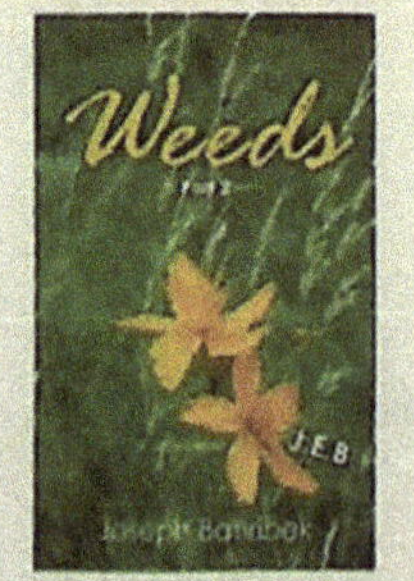

Weeds: Part 2
by Joseph Bahribek | Oct 10, 2022
Paperback
$12.99
✓prime
FREE delivery Sep 6 - 11 on $25 of items shipped by Amazon
Or fastest delivery Sep 4 - 8

My Dears
As you been Seeing
In this page it is
Quiet Bit; Listed
Book From my publishing
Book, they located on
Alot location and
on Amazon
J*E*B*
[illegible]

الأعزاء
شاهد على هذه
الصفحة قليل من
تأليفاتي من تأليفي
في عدد من مواقع
وفي موقع أمازون.
ج*ا*ب

50

My Dears
IE Will Comes New Book
From my publishing
Title: Look Like
Real Leaves - Weed-
J*E*B*

الأعزائي : سوف يأتي
كتاب جديد من تأليفي
يبدو أوراق حقيقية WeedBook

⊐*٩*ل *⊿*۴*ع*

INTRODUCTION

To All Deares Womens offspring
of Eve Rip of Adam
Hi My Deares Womens Reader This
Book is my gifts to All of you
(O, pretty Eden Earth FLwores))
My Evolutation For you All: GOD
Creat you from Side or From RIP
of Adam: meaning word: Adam: -
is Eartly + Blood + Spirit of GOD =
Adam: Become Life
my Deares Eve, in my Term and my opinion
my Understanding offspring off EVE they
Are Different than man From, From Ability
and body of Eve is Very pretty and Sensitive
to be hurt. From Toch, her feeling By the
Word and By hurt? And I Will Writing
my feelin and motion my Good Words
Toward the Eve? I konw my feeling
this Book Will suprise you and you will
Love It. Introduce my Self for you Not
For Friendshap With you? But for my
Respect For you Eve? you Are the
Samgenetic Im Human Being and
She is As part of my body GOD Creat you
From my RIP my Flash? that Way the Eve
Very Important in This Century Eve
is the Right hand? Eve She is my
Dignity and my honor That Way I Wold
Like to Wright my Good Word For
Eve For my Respect For her? I Will
Repeat my Word For you Adam
to you As you Love your Soul and
Respeted? do the Same For EVE
As you know Eve is Very Sensitive
to be hurt For hurt her Feeling? the
Eve is As the Flowers of feild
the Are As Brunch of thee As
you Are? All Women they
Are Very pretty they Need
your Help you know your
self the Are Weakar than you
I Will All Way Repat my Word
For you Respect and Love EVE As
GOD Creat her from you
Rip and your   As Brunch
of Tree As you See That and
Also you Want be Alone your
self? in This Century Eve
As your Right hand As I
Said Eve All Way Stand
Side by Said of you.
O: Adam Thank you.

Age. 71y.